THE STRANGER WITHIN

by
JENNIFER DETLEFSEN

BOOK
ONE

CONTENTS

AMANDA

Amanda walked down the narrow, crowded street in the Muslim sector of the city. She kept her head down and avoided eye contact, although she peered greedily at every movement the other Muslim women made, trying hard to emulate them and not draw attention to herself. It was only when she walked into one of the little stores packed tightly with imported goods in every available space, and actually bought something, that it sometimes became tricky. She'd hand over the money and the person behind the counter would get a glimpse of her light coloured eyes that she tried to hide under the burqa, but she wasn't always successful. They would peer at her curiously, and though they never ventured an outright question, they watched her suspiciously until she left the shop. She was used to this reaction now though, and just ignored it, hurriedly moving out of the shop if she thought the keeper was becoming too interested or agitated. She didn't want to draw any unnecessary attention to herself in case someone had a bad reaction.

Surprisingly though, she'd quickly become quite adept at mingling with the other Muslim women and most ignored her. And more surprising to herself, she very quickly became comfortable with being this anonymous woman, covered from head to toe, shopping, going about her business, like the other women did. Or so it must seem to them, that that was what she was doing.

But it had not always been so. As she browsed from

shop to shop, she reflected on the time six months ago, when she first thought of the idea of putting on a burka. At first she laughed at herself and of course thought the idea was preposterous, but it stayed with her and she played with the idea in her mind. She'd picture herself wearing it unashamedly, walking down the street with it on, she just wanted to try it, feel what it was like. She thought in the beginning that she would never dare do it, but after a while she talked herself into it. She'd taken a couple of months to properly formulate the idea and then work up the courage to carry it out, and her family were still none the wiser; hopefully they never would be.

It had started with the marmalade. She hated marmalade, with its enticing bright orange colouring, promising a sweet sensation as you imagined it touching your tongue, only to find that it was bitter, terribly bitter, no sweetness at all. It was the same with black coffee. Without that small hint of sugar, it just tasted bitter, horrible.

Amanda's' husband Neil, didn't know it, but lately she'd been watching him through the corner of her eye. He'd been doing the usual; eating his toast with orange marmalade, sipping his sugarless black espresso while reading his paper at the breakfast table or sitting in his leather recliner after dinner, reading his latest novel, usually a biography or a war story, his spectacles perched precariously near the tip of his nose.

She thought he looked ridiculously funny except for the fact that he wasn't. It troubled her that he took himself so seriously, and it troubled her that she was changing, and he wasn't. It troubled her a great deal, and what was more worrying was that he didn't seem to notice the rift, the empty space that was ever widening between them.

The kids, with their uncanny ability to instantly identify the obvious, they noticed. Only Lukie of the two boys, noticed enough or wasn't preoccupied enough to say something.

"Hey mum, you and Dad never do anything together anymore." He'd say it in passing, not realising the significance.

"I know darling, we're both busy."

So she'd watch him. At first when they were married she was bemused by his repetitive habits and quirky nuances. But twenty years down the track she began to despise his predictable actions, his individual mannerisms, the way he would sometimes clear his throat just before he folded his newspaper and rise from the table after a meal. The way he'd annoyingly rub his hand through his thick locks of hair when he was thinking about something; hair thicker than it should have been at his age.

He was still ruggedly handsome for a man in his fifties, taller than most, his physique kept strong with regular bouts of squash with his work colleagues, and the weekends spent playing golf. She'd notice younger women at the supermarket or the restaurant where they occasionally went out to dinner, glancing at him, but he never noticed. But for her, his attractiveness had long ago waned, dissipated. With the advent of time, he'd become too familiar, too constant, another regular facet of her daily life, like the train she caught to work, and the regular faces she'd see sitting in the same seats every day.

Once she thought that might be the problem. She spoke to Neil about it.

"Maybe I've been doing the same thing for too long. Perhaps I need a change, a new career."

But he was always the voice of reason, "Well, that may be the case. But before you make a radical decision, change something else, something smaller, first and see if you still feel the same. A new hobby or a new sport. Just take it slow before you decide. You don't have to work at all if you don't want to, you know that." He smiled and kissed her forehead. "See you tonight," he said cheerily as he strode out the door. She didn't feel like smiling.

So she changed her routine to include a yoga class after work and then she found she enjoyed work again.

Neil was always right. She used to admire that in him. In the beginning his calm demeanour was never ruffled by her immature tantrums, "After all," he'd always say, "you're so much younger than I am." He'd say it in a complimentary way rather than condescending, as if he was the amused parent watching a toddler tantrum, repeating that he was so lucky to have "caught" her; the age difference being nearly thirteen years. And later he was always the calming presence with the children, assuaging arguments and deflecting hurt feelings.

Her parents didn't approve at first, due to the large age difference. He was only seven years younger than her own father, but by the time her father died suddenly of a heart attack at the age of fifty seven, they'd become best mates. She knew her father visited them more to see her husband than herself, they played golf together and on occasion had lunch or dinner together, just the two of them. She tried to ignore the fact that her father liked her husband better than he liked his own daughter, but it irked her. There was always that uncomfortable feeling of having unfinished business with her father, but he and Neil pretended everything was fine. Neil seemed more upset than she was when he died.

She'd had a patchy relationship at best with her father; her older sister Christine, was the favourite, the successful lawyer. His first daughter was pretty and witty, and demanded attention. With Amanda he'd had to make do with a mediocre daughter who had a mediocre career, an ex hairdresser who eventually qualified as a nurse in aged care. Amanda found her job immensely satisfying and resumed it again once both her children were settled in school; but she could never compete with the wild tales of the courtroom with which her childless older sister entertained her enthralled father. Amanda's' stories, consisting mainly of her children's achievements in school, just didn't seem to compare, and he was never really interested in the children. He could be nasty at times, and she decided early on to shield the children as much as possible from his, what would only be in her opinion, a negative influence.

Amanda's mother was the compliant wife of an overbearing and sometimes domineering husband. He had a sharp verbal wit and kept the best lambaste for his wife. It inevitably occurred at the dinner table, her father rising up in victory with a sneering grin on his face, at times with a searing look in his wife's dejected direction, at times not even the need to dispense a look; her mother shrinking in her chair, her conversation equivocally garrotted. Amanda imminently shrank with her, and politely rose to clear the dishes. Her mother was generally quiet, and family friends always said Amanda took after her mother, but she knew they were all just fulfilling their dutiful roles within the family hierarchy.

After her father died Amanda knew her mother was lonely. They visited each other as often as possible but they could not evolve from the characters of martyr and resentful accomplice, and the visits from Christine to either of them were rare. When her mother became ill with various ailments, Amanda became the martyr, feigning sympathy she really didn't feel, for ailments she wasn't sure she believed in; sacrificing time for herself and the children to ferry her mother to and from the doctor, or to and from the hospital, and thereafter cooking for her, and her and Neil maintaining her house, as well as their own. Her mother was always sick with something, she always had been, and Amanda was sure it must be annoying even to her doctors, of which she had a few. Amanda was sure she was a bit of a hypochondriac, and that was why she was dubious at times about her mother's symptoms.

This went on for years until her mother succumbed to an extended bout of pneumonia, and infection in hospital and subsequently died after a particularly prolonged admittance cycle.

When her mother died, Amanda felt a mixture of relief, guilt and regret. Whenever she thought of her mother the same feelings would return, as potently as ever, so she'd put them out of her mind. She never mentioned her feelings to Neil, and he never asked; it was a disregarded topic.

Amanda had begun to shrink back when Neil routinely kissed her hello or goodbye or went to touch her during the course of a normal day. When she realised what she was doing she made a conscious effort not to do so. She feigned normality and moved forward to peck him on the lips in return or give a warm hug as he did, but she didn't feel the warmth that was supposed to accompany them. Instead she felt icy cold. She also started to pull away from his touch in their bed, and began rising early and retiring late, after she knew he'd already fallen asleep, to avoid the intimacy she'd begun to dread. Sometimes she felt ashamed and pitied him for something he knew nothing of and she was annoyed with herself over her petulant behaviour, but she couldn't help it. She just did not want him to touch her anymore.

Either he didn't seem to notice or he wasn't concerned, but Neil did not mention the change. Or perhaps it was such a slow change that he just accepted it. Regardless, he was not the type to make a fuss; he would simply wait for her behaviour to return to normal.

So Amanda had begun to watch him. She was trying to figure out what she'd found so attractive about him all those years ago, but she couldn't see anything that would have attracted her now. He just seemed boring.

She knew he was a handsome man, but that couldn't have been all. There had been plenty of good looking men around. Amanda met Neil when she was studying Geriatric Nursing at the University of California. He was a college professor and well admired by the female students she studied with. He was mature and studious compared to the other fun loving men around her and she knew she liked that about him at the time. Was she replacing an emotionally distant father, as the psychologists would have us believe? She didn't know. He was tall, handsome and wiser than her male peers, and like a lot of the other girls nursed a crush on Professor Neil Hendley. Surprising to her, he seemed to take a liking to her, and after two years of mild debates over coffee he finally asked her out. They became an item fairly quickly and were married within five years of meeting. They were a quiet couple and well liked in their circles, but because of the age difference between herself and the other wives in Neils peer group, she didn't feel she fit in that well; while she was having babies, their children were already beginning to take flight.

They were more like grandmothers, and some were closer to her mothers age than her own, so they didn't mix with them very often. Neil didn't seem to mind, always buried in books or his work, and Amanda had her own friends closer to her own age.

From the outside it may have looked difficult, but the marriage had been a successful one. Only until recently, when Amanda had begun having negative thoughts about her life.

These feelings about her life came on suddenly, it was not like it was a slow process for her of realising over time that she was unhappy. It was more like one day she woke up to find that she hated her life, and herself, and the forboding feelings that she had did not go away. After she noticed it for the first time, she woke up with the same feeling, the same way every morning, and it got worse with time.

She did not tell anyone about it and berated herself for feeling this way; she continued on with her life as if everything was the same for a long time. But eventually, after many months, she moved into a dark place and her family couldn't help but start to notice.

TRAIN TRAVELLING

Amanda was becoming bolder. Every morning as she sat on the train on her way to work, she thought about her secret life of crime that went on afterwards. And at work she was preoccupied with the excited feeling she had about what she was doing, and would glance at her watch all afternoon and hurry towards her locker as soon as the dial touched five. She'd never done that before.

Amanda wanted to find out what it was like to wear the burka. But now she sat on the morning train and wondered if she had the courage to wear the full habit on the train. She turned from gazing unseeing out of the glazed train window, her mind racing over the activities she had planned for the afternoon, and looked up at the faces surrounding her.

She studied furtively the youngish girl sitting opposite her. With her white crisp shirt and smart black jacket and pants, would she be offended or even repulsed by a women wearing a head dress sitting across from her? Would the Caucasian men in the train find it distasteful? Would she even encounter some vitriol, or even some kind of attack? She decided that she didn't care. And the only reason for that, she knew, was because no one would know it was her dressed up, she would be anonymous. And that thought excited her even more. If she could work up the courage to do what she wanted to do, to put the burka on and go out in public as if she was a real Muslim, she would feel elated. No longer would she be just Amanda, the rejected daughter, the dutiful wife, but someone covered up, unrecognisable, a different person completely.

But she wasn't a real Muslim, she was just pretending. And there came the guilt again. If she'd genuinely converted to the Islam faith, she would have the right to wear the religious garment and she wouldn't have any reason to feel guilty, but that wasn't the case. It was a joke to her really, some fun, an adventure that she'd conjured up for herself and decided to carry out; it made her chuckle inwardly but she wondered could there be any adverse repercussions for what she was thinking of doing? Would Muslims be incensed if they knew someone was pretending to be one of them? Probably, they were very sensitive about their religion, easily offended. The ones she'd seen on the news were, anyway. But again, no one knew her and she could do what she liked. This was America after all, not a Muslim country, and basically she could wear anything she liked, there was nothing anyone could do to stop her, it wasn't against the law to wear a burka, or a bikini or anything else in between. And this was part of the fascination. The fact that the body covering was as much a uniform to Muslim women as the bikini was to Caucasian American women. The irony of this fascinated her and she couldn't get it out of her mind. Why were these two type of women so different? Of course they were a product of their environment, the culture they were born into, but what she really wanted to find out was whether the Muslim women thought differently to her, a typical American woman, or did they have secret hopes and dreams of freedom from their religion and their culture? Did they wish they had been born a Caucasian and had the freedoms of Caucasian women?

So she justified her actions and worked up the nerve to put on the garment and carry out her plan, which was to mix with the Muslim women and try to find out what they're lives were really like. She decided her first experiment would be a day trip to the city centre on the train. The more people there were around, the easier it would be to mingle unnoticed and she needed that.

It took her a few times before she had found the resolve to venture out in public and then onto a train to take her to the city. She planned to do it after work, it was easier, as she was already away from her neighborhood where no one would recognise her and no one would miss her because she told Neil that she was working late. She was ashamed of herself, and Neil would be horrified, that she'd started frequenting the public toilets, but it was the only place she could change anonymously. They were dirty, putrid places and she was frightened to use them, but they were a necessary part of her plan, and she chose the safest and cleanest one she could find, in the busiest part of town.

The first time she pulled the black cloth over her head, she felt ridiculous. It was one thing to parade about in the private bedroom of her house but it was quite another to actually step out into the street with it on. She fussed with the material and sat on the toilet seat for nearly an hour before she turned the silver lock on the door that she'd been staring at, and stumbled out, thinking that everyone outside was suddenly staring at her and knew she was pretending. But they didn't stare actually, the people were all busy going wherever they were going, and so she cheered up, and delightedly headed for the appropriate platform.

But on the train it was different. It didn't happen every time she was on the train, but occasionally she would come across the obvious disapproval of some people. And when this happened, she wasn't really prepared for the attention as much as she'd thought she was. She moved uncomfortably in her seat or sat still, frozen when different people repeatedly glanced her way, or sometimes stared aggressively, deliberately trying to meet her eyes. She averted them always, staring at the window unwaveringly. But by the time she arrived at the correct station she'd been joined by other women wearing the garment, and so she relaxed, fitting in well, and followed them out the doors.

This was the part she enjoyed. This part of the city was busy, like any other. Muslims going about their business like everyone else, shopping, talking, laughing, hurrying children along, the men and women standing around in groups.

So this is what it was like. Covered from head to toe, no one knowing what you looked or felt like underneath. It was strangely liberating for her to be anonymous, but she was acutely aware of the irony that it really was not liberating for Islam women to wear the garment.

So she strolled around the precinct, browsing at the unfamiliar items of food and utensils in the shops, thoroughly enjoying the experience. She continued her expeditions a couple of days per week and became much more confortable in her anomolous clothing.

One day as she was browsing over some interesting spices she was startled.

"What are you cooking?"

Amanda was at first disconcerted, no one had ever spoken to her before except to grunt briefly when she paid a shopkeeper for something she'd bought.

"Um," she hesitated because she thought if she didn't say something authentically Muslim she'd be caught out. Then she began to panic, 'What do they eat, it has to be halal doesn't it?', but then she collected herself and decided to stall.

"I haven't decided yet", she smiled convincingly at the woman addressing her, wearing the same black abaya as she was. The woman looked about the same age as herself, pretty and wearing makeup. She had friendly, inquisitive eyes and Amanda warmed to her instantly.

"I'm making Biryani," the woman commented, "nothing interesting tonight." She paused as she picked up some coriander, mint and cashews. "Are you visiting the mosque?" She glanced up briefly.

"Ah, yes I am, the mosque." Amanda nodded her head to give her words more gravity. "I think I'll cook Biryani as well." She moved to pick up the same ingredients. "Do you have a good recipe?" She could now look at the woman without seeming like she was staring. She could hardly contain her excitement at having a conversation with the woman and tried to think hard at ways of prolonging it.

"Yes, I have my own method, I vary the meat or the nuts or

even the oil. Do you do that?"

"Yes, I do, all the time, it's a very versatile recipe."

"Are you going to the five o'clock prayer?"

"Yes, I'm just on my way there now." Amanda turned away and bit her lip with the lie, but she desperately wanted to get to know some Muslim women and she was not going to let this opportunity pass by.

"We'll go together then. I'm Aleyah, nice to meet you." Aleyah smiled her amiable smile again and Amanda felt like she may have found a friend.

"Amanda, nice to meet you." She smiled warmly in return and followed her new friend out of the shop.

  Amanda kept pace with Aleyah and tried to keep the conversation all about her new friend. She asked her questions about herself without seeming rude or intrusive, and found that Aleyah had come from Turkey with her parents when she was five years old. By the time she was eighteen she was engaged and by twenty she was married. Now at twenty three she's just found out she was pregnant. She seemed excited and Amanda remembered the feeling. This was something she could share and she spoke about how it felt to have a baby, how her boys had grown so quickly and how they now seemed to no longer need her.

  Amanda went to prayer in the nearby temple but although she had enjoyed meeting the friendly Aleyah she never returned, and never wore the full burkah again. She felt foolish and disparaging pretending to be one of the Muslim women and never did it again.

FRANK MARTINEZ

Frank Martinez had just visited his mother in the nursing home. He visited her every week and it took up nearly the whole of every Saturday to do it. Two hours there, two hours back and an hour sitting by her bed, or wheeling her outside in her wheelchair to sit in the sun. She had been diagnosed with schizophrenia early in his childhood and had been in and out of hospital ever since. A lot of the time she hardly knew who he was, but seeing she was the only family he had left, he clung to the only feeling of belonging he'd ever had.

He was mainly brought up by his immigrant father, who worked long hours as a construction worker, and had a bad temper at the best of times. He would beat Frank regularly, and otherwise they did not see much of each other, outside of the meager meals his father would irregularly dish up around his drinking schedule.

When his father died two weeks after Franks' eleventh birthday he was more relieved than anything else. He went to live with his uncle and generally got beaten up by his older cousins. Nothing really changed for him.

Frank was an only child, like his mother had been. His father, mother, and uncle were born in Mexico, but he was born after they came to the US on temporary work visas and never went back. Frank and his cousins were US citizens. In his mothers rare lucid moments she would lecture him about how lucky he was to live in a country with such opportunity. But he never felt lucky. He was a quiet under-achiever at school and after reading his reports, his intoxicated father would slowly undo his belt buckle and whack him with it all over, shouting at him in his slurry deep mexican accent, swearing at him in his native spanish, and chasing him out of the house. He left school at the earliest opportunity. His uncle got him a job with his cousins at the local shipyard and he never tried to work anywhere else.

Instead, he and his cousins became part of the local Logan Heights gang, a notorious gang of the San Diego area, with strong links to the drug trafficking and murderous gang the Tijuana Cartel across the border in Mexico. The fights were vicious and deadly, there were drugs, lots of money, and murders. You would travel alone at your own peril, but Frank and his cousins soon became streetwise in the gang, and owned the streets, at times the gang was four hundred strong. Rival gang members were killed without hesitation, and the more murders you committed, the higher you ranked in the gang. And when there was nothing else to do they travelled to other areas looking for trouble. They would engage the blacks and gangs all the way up the coast to Los Angeles and the opposite way into Mexico. And when they were really bored they would pick on ethnic groups like the Muslims or the jews. The Muslims were particularly hated, the strange men with the towels on their heads, and the women, covered from head to toe with that odd black garment. They were easy pickings and kept the gang amused. They would hang around outside the small temples and follow the young men until they were relatively alone and beat them, pulling the head covers off, and pulling them around by their long hair and beards. They would particularly harass the mexican Islam converts, beating the men and tormenting the women.

Frank Martinez was now fifty two years old. The days of his youthful gangbanging were long gone and he was angry. He'd been angry all his life, as long as he could remember. He was angry at his mother, who married a brute and then got sick; his father, who was nothing but a brute; his uncle, who couldn't remember his name; and the cousins who used to beat him up all the time, the fact that he couldn't even rank high in the gang, and was regularly beaten up by the other gang members, much to the amusement of his pitiless cousins. He particularly remembered his initiation ceremony at eleven years old; he was blindfolded and then beaten to a pulp, before a gun was put in his hand and he was told to do his first 187, which if he hadn't carried out he would have been done himself.

He was angry at his school and his teachers, where he was in trouble all the time and just didn't fit in, and was eventually expelled for punching a female teacher in the face. He was angry that he'd had the same job for thirty years and had nothing to show for it. But most of all he was angry at the shiny white people with their big houses and big brand new cars, only a few kilometres from where he lived. And he hated the immigrants. The odd jews with their long dresses and conical hats, walking around always with a Torah in their hands. The blacks with their long shorts, stolen Nike runners and loud music controlling the street corners in the city; and the Muslim freaks, the men with their towelled heads and the women covered head to toe in the black robes. All these people kept their heads down or looked away when he came near them, passing them in the street, and his father pumped into him that anyone who didn't look you in the eye was suspicious. No, he didn't trust them, they were different and they were hiding something in their suspicious eyes, or maybe they hated him as much as he hated them. Anyway, any look at all was enough to get them in trouble with the gang when they were young, and sometimes he wished he still had his gang around to teach these intruders a lesson.

Every time he saw them his hatred would well up in him as he knocked off work and walked to his regular watering hole. He drank heavily and muttered to himself or anyone that would listen, only leaving as the doors thudded closed behind him, always the last customer.

He had no one to go home to. He never married although he'd come as close as he was capable of once. His uncle died and his cousins were either dead, in jail, and the remaining two eventually cut all ties with the criminals and the old life, had married, had children and moved on.

Frank , in his twenties, had eventually moved into the bungalow at the back of his mothers house, who now had twenty four hour carers appointed by the local county. He went back to work at the shipyard and spent his spare time drinking like his father had. When he visited his surviving two cousins, he found he wasn't welcome. Their wives saw him as trouble, connected to the gangs, and didn't want him around. Finally he stopped visiting altogether.

He had a sort of girlfriend once. He knew Sonja from school and she seemed to take a liking to him, but at that time he only had eyes for someone else. But one day, when he was about twenty eight, he came across her again, and she invited herself over to his house. For a couple of years they drank together, and slept together, and she would cook him meals on the weekend when she wasn't working.

At times they would fight and he wouldn't see her for a couple of weeks and then she'd come back again like nothing had happened. Then one day she announced that she was marrying an old boyfriend. She slept with him one more time and then he never saw her again. He wondered sometimes if he should have asked her to marry him but the subject never came up. He thought about her sometimes, when he was sitting alone at the bar, but by the next morning he had already forgotten about her again. By this time his mother had been admitted to the closest available nursing home and he moved back into the main house. But it was a lonely dark, dilapidated house, and he went there only to sleep.

Frank sat at the bar with the usual angry scowl on his dark, dirty face and grunted at the barman whenever he needed a refill. He drank whisky, dry, one after the other, but his system had become so accustomed to the drink that it had no effect, and anyway his personality didn't change no matter what the influence, drink, women or anything else. He was always a disgruntled customer, and the bartender knew better than to refuse his repeated requests for another, hour after hour; he wasn't the drink police after all. Occasionally he felt sorry for this lonely figure always perched at the end of the counter at 6.00pm on the dot, but that pity soon disintegrated whenever anyone was unfortunate enough to have a short interaction with Frank. It would be short, and it always ended badly, for the injured object of Franks attention, or for Frank sobering up in the local lockup until the early hours of the morning, and for him, the barman, cleaning in Franks wake. Yes the local law enforcement knew Frank well, from the early years of his gang associations, though they'd never got him for a serious crime, they knew he was a member of the gangs; and now to his latter year short term incarcerations, mainly for drunkenness and barfights.

  And tonight was shaping up to be one of those nights. This guy just doesn't know when to shut up, the barman was thinking. He tried repeatedly to move the man away from Frank, or hint that he should give it a rest but his attempts went unappreciated. The guy went on and on about the attack on the twin towers in New York. It was one year old news now but someone had brought up the subject.

"Those bastard Muslims, they'll get theirs one day, who do they think they are, coming to America and killing Americans, damn bastards!" He downed another shot of whiskey and banged the glass down on the worn wood. "Lets have another!" He motioned to the barman, swaying. He then made the mistake of slapping Frank on the back, "What do ya think of those mozzies, buddy?"

The poor man was lying on his back on the floor before he knew what hit him. "You better get outta here Frank." The barman shook his head.

Frank moved towards the door, and waved his hand

dismissively, "Yeah."
 Frank walked along the road rubbing his knuckles where he'd hit the man in the bar. They were red and sore, and that made him feel angrier than he usually did. That's when he noticed the Muslim man walking about a block ahead of him. 'What's under that stupid towel on his head', Frank thought angrily and stepped up his pace. He'd been drinking quite a bit so he couldn't catch up that fast, but by the end of the next block Frank was on top of him.
"What ya got under that towel, Mahoun?" The Latinos called every Muslim 'Mahoun' or a group of them 'Mozzies'. "Why don't you show me!" In that moment Frank was reliving what he and his cousins did in the past, where he was accepted and looked on as one of the gang, and this was not a request. In the next instant he'd pulled the turban off and grabbed the man by his hair and slammed him into the brick fence beside the footpath. Frank's strength was astounding for a man in his early fifties, and he still thought nothing of attacking a perceived foe. For a moment he realises his attack doesn't feel as good as it used to when he was young, but quickly forgets again. He briefly looks down at the man lying unmoving on the cold grey concrete and kicks him in the stomach. He then continues walking and slowly makes his way home.

AMANDA'S ACCIDENT

Amanda's world was collapsing around her, and she felt helpless to stop it. In fact she knew that she was the saboteur, the conductor who started this train running and continued to fuel the engine. She'd started something unwillingly, almost imperceptibly, and now she could not control the feelings that welled in her consciousness and dominated her psyche. These feelings of loathing of her own life, her own family, past and present; her mother, the helpless enabler that allowed her father to dominate them all; her father, the nasty bully of whom she could not even bare to think of; her sister who could apparently do no wrong. And then there was her own family of whom her feelings towards them she felt ashamed. Her husband Neil, a great and understanding man, who could not understand why she did not get along with her father, the way he did, and therefore in perpetuating a close relationship with him, did not realise how much he alienated his wife. Her sons, whom she loved and was so close to when they were young, but now simply, just did not need her anymore. She should be lauding their newfound independence, encouraging them at the beginning of their lives, but instead she resented their increasing autonomy.

She'd started having panic attacks. All of a sudden it seemed she would be thinking too much, dwelling on one particular destructive subject and it would begin. She might be on the train travelling towards home at the end of the day, or cooking dinner in the kitchen, when all of a sudden she would feel claustrophobic, even if she was out in the open somewhere, and she felt like she needed to run away but there was nowhere to run to. Her breathing would become rapid and she felt like her head was about to explode. She would look from side to side as if looking for an escape, but there was none. Her eyes would be wide-eyed and scared, she was basically near hysterical.

The episodes only lasted a minute but they distressed her immensely. For the rest of the day she would be anxious and exhausted, slightly disconcerted. She would start to walk into a room and then forget why she'd gone in there. She'd start to chop onions and forget what she'd planned to cook. She'd start a sentence and forget what she was about to say. In fact she thought at times that she was losing her mind.

But these episodes were short lived and she did not put much stock in them. She knew that what she was actually suffering from was depression. She did not need to be diagnosed to know that there was a constant, dark cloud hanging over her head that she could not shake. It coloured grey her whole world, and everything that she would have once taken delight in, it
tainted. In the spring when the bright white and yellow daisies flowed out through the diamond shapes of the wire fencing in the suburban streetscapes, she would take such joy in their perfectly shaped petals and their burst of life. She remembered acutely that feeling of joy and then was doubly saddened by the fact now that that feeling was only a memory.

She could not replicate that feeling anymore, she could only admire the flowers as if seeing them from a distance or as you would in a picture. Everything now in her life she saw as flawed in some way, as if every decision she had ever made had been wrong, or for the wrong reason.

And she knew exactly when the depression had started. Years ago two things happened that changed her perspective on the world she lived in. At first her despondent and pessimistic feelings were inperceptible, but they gradually increased until by now they were ruling her life.

Amanda awoke to find faces peering at her closely, and muffled voices slowly became intelligible. "Are you alright darling?" She recognised Neil and his concerned features, and then she remembered – she'd been in a car accident. She looked around and realised she was lying in a hospital bed. "How long have I been here?" She tried to sit up but immediately felt pain in her head. Her hands flew up to her temples at the pain.

"No, no just relax, you have a concussion that's all." The nurse pushed her gently back down into the pillows. "Just a bit of rest and you'll be good as new," she said smiling.

  Amanda knew the drill and also knew that she could not be released until the doctor visited her and approved it. She was a nurse herself after all. So she sat back onto the surprisingly comfortable bed and repeated her question.

"How long have I been here?'

"Only a couple of hours honey, they gave you a sedative to sleep." Neil spoke reassuringly.

"Do the boys know?"

"Not yet, I thought I'd wait, see how you were first."

"Don't tell them, it's not necessary for them to worry." Neil heard the anxiety in her voice.

"Ok, ok, we won't tell them yet, but they will need to know later."

"I'm so sleepy," and with that she turned slightly sideways and went back to sleep.

  Once Amanda returned from the hospital later that day, Neil told her he had some adverse news to tell her.

"I'm sorry you're not feeling the best darling, but you need to know that your father died this morning while you were in hospital. I wanted to tell you earlier of course but I really wanted to make sure you were up to it after the accident. I'm sorry love, I really am."

He held her close but the close proximity felt stifling, and she pushed him away.

She recognised his concern though, and strangely reassured

him instead.

"It wasn't unexpected Neil, don't worry."

Her father had been unwell now for the last six months after a sudden stroke, and they had been expecting the worse any day.

She went through the motions of looking after her mother and sister who came to stay during the following few days before the funeral, and then insisted her mother stay for a couple more months, now that she was alone at home.

Even though she was the younger sister, she had always had to be the responsible one as her older sister was always busy with her work and career to have anything to do with the practicle aspects of looking after family. It was Amanda who visited her parents regularly and made sure they grew into aging without any problems. It was of course expected of her, because she was a nurse by profession, but she still resented it at times.

Eventually her mother decided to go back home even though Neil insisted that she should stay on at their house permanently in the back guest area of the house but she decided not to, much to Amanda's relief. Her mother always had a way of making other people feel sorry for her, that somehow she made it seem that she was hard done by in life, but Amanda had not sympathy for her. She had chosen to marry her husband, Amanda's father, and Amanda blamed her for never being able to stand up to him when he bullied them.

So everyone else saw Amanda's mother as a kind, gentle woman, and a good wife, but Amanda knew that she also had a harder side that Amanda felt the full brunt of growing up, and her parents stuck together when it came to corporal punishment.

Amanda didn't really feel very much at all over her father's passing, and she became busy as the sole caregiver of her needy, helpless mother, as well as continuing her roles as wife and mother and her job as a nurse, so she didn't have time to give it much thought.

But unconsciously she did not realise that it would be the catalyst that changed her perception of a reasonably happy life into one that she could not see any good in at all, and one that would that would start her family on a journey from which they would never recover.

FRANK'S INITIATION

Frank had just turned 11. As he was being blindfolded he was telling himself to be strong. He'd seen initiations before and some were more brutal than others, but this gang, the Logan Heights gang, was particularly merciless.

He hoped his wouldn't be too bad although he knew it was going to hurt. What he didn't realise was how much. He could hear his cousins laughing and smirking while someone pushed him around but he wasn't ready for the first blow. It hit him square in the back of his head and he fell flat on his face on the hard concrete. He was immediately pulled up by his arms and let go. He tried to stand and was about to fall when he felt more blows, on his back, his arms and his legs, and he toppled to the ground helplessly.

He desperately wanted to become a member, to join his cousins and finally get their respect and acceptance. He thought that if he proved to them that he could be a powerful member of the gang they'd finally accept him, instead of berating and beating him all the time. And he needed their protection and this was the only way to get it. If they ever rejected him, leaving him alone and exposed on the streets, he'd be an easy target for the rival gangs and even the blacks on the outskirts of the gangs territory. He could also become a target for Logan Heights members who knew he'd been rejected. He thought this would be the turning point of his life. Those guys had lots of money, lots of drugs, they had guns, and they had respect. He knew he had to do this but he wasn't prepared to be beaten within an inch of his life by his own cousins.

His cousins and other members of the gang began the beating by using sticks and planks that had been ripped out of someone's garden fence. They hit him around the head and back and legs until he fell, but when he lay on the ground, they began kicking him over and over again until he finally lost conciousness. They then walked away and left him there, unconscious and bleeding. Everyone knew better than to be perceived as trying to help him or they'd be set upon. Not that anyone cared. If you survived the beating you were in; and if you didn't you were dead.

Frank woke up on the pavement the next day and wished he hadn't. He felt pain all over his body and couldn't move. He looked at his hand lying on the pavement near his face and he could see his twisted fingers where they'd been broken trying to shield his head. He tried to lean on his arms and lift himself up but he screamed in pain as he put his weight on his shoulder and knew he had some fractured bones everywhere. He blinked his eyes because he couldn't see properly and realised his face must be swollen.

It was then his cousins lifted him up by his arms. He screamed in pain.

"Ey the boys made it!"

"How ya feelin' homie!"

They sat him against the concrete pillar of the overpass. Frank started feeling dizzy and began wretching. With every heave his whole body ached but his cousins just laughed.

"C'mon man, you're thru, get up, we have a job for you man."

They pulled him up and started walking him down the road. He could hardly walk but they kept pulling him along and it seemed they walked a long time, but they'd only gone a couple of blocks.

A car pulled up beside them, screeching quickly to a halt and they threw him in the back seat and then climbed in on top of him.

Frank felt the worst he ever had. His whole body ached and he could hardly see through his swollen eyes. He couldn't talk due to his swollen mouth, and the cuts on his lips smarted when he tried to lick them. He lay on the back seat where his cousins had thrown him and couldn't move.

"Hey take this bro', you'll feel better." His cousin put a pill in his mouth and then poured some water down his throat. Frank coughed and choked but the pill went down. The car drove on and in about ten minutes Frank started to feel a warm sensation flow through his body. The pain left and he attempted to sit up.

"Hey you feelin' better man!", his cousin slapped his back and put a gun in his hand. "What do ya think of that baby?!" His cousin stared at the gun with big loving eyes and wore a grin that filled his whole face. "She's yours, homie, you one of us now, aint she sweet?" He lovingly nodded at the small pistol that now rested across his palm. Frank had never held a gun before and it was heavy. The golden metal shined brilliantly in his eyes.

"It's boodiful aint it?! A .38 El Presidente compliments of the la chota! Go on try it!" His cousin held the gun out the window and pulled the trigger. The gunshot rang in Franks ears. "Go on try it!"

Frank wasn't sure what his cousin meant about the gun coming from the local police, either they'd killed some or they'd been given the guns, but either way he suddenly felt powerful.

He held up the gun at first shakily, and then with a firmer grip pulled the trigger. Everyone in the car yelled in approval, including the two essa in the front seats that he didn't know, and then everyone got serious.

"Hey cuz, ya gonna do a job now. It's the last one prove you can be one of us. Now you take that baby and you pop the dude I show you. OK?"

Frank knew this was no time to be squeamish. If he didn't do this, he knew he would be the one to die. "Ok."

They drove for about two hours to L.A. It was dark by now and they parked in an alleyway between buildings. They all got out and walked to a club with a sign out the front saying Leonardos. The guy who had been driving walked up to the biggest man at the door and slipped something into his hand, then walking straight past him into the club. They all followed. The music was loud and the coloured lights flickered this way and that. They stood in a dark corner of the club for what seemed like hours, watching the girls gyrating to the music and the men getting drunk. They didn't drink at all.

"Hey." The driver sidled up to Frank and whispered in his ear. Frank was surprised, the esse had ignored him until now. "You see that hombre with the red and blue cap?" He nodded towards a group of men on the other side of some tables, sitting on the lounges against the dark burgundy wall.

"Sure, I see him." Frank was feeling unusually bold and reckless.

The drivers head came down close to him. "You follow him into el bano, and you pop him right in the face, you got that?" For the first time he looked Frank straight in the eyes, as if to gauge any hesitation.

But there was none. Frank gripped the heat tighter under his jacket and went to move. He felt the drivers hand firmly grip his arm. "Esperar. Wait."

It seemed like more hours went by, and suddenly the guy with the hat got up and moved towards the latrines. The driver pinched Franks arm painfully, and Frank sprung into action. He caught up to the guy in the cap by pushing people out of his way. He ended up right behind him but the guy didn't notice. The guy walked straight into a cubicle and turned to close the door but Frank blocked the way. He already had the gun out and shot the guy right in the face just like the driver had told him to. He walked quickly to the basin and washed the blood off his face, then pushed his way out of the toilets with everyone else. He then casually walked back to his gang and they all filed slowly out the front door.

NEIL

Neil walked determinedly into his study and sat down at his desk. He could think in here. He rubbed his hands over the soft leather arms of his chair and felt satisfaction at the beauty of the instrument. He admired the handsome shine of the gloss on his pure oak desk, the splendour of the timber filling his heart with pride. This room was his domain in the house, his sanctuary; they all had one, the boys had their rooms, as individual as they were; the older Aaron, with his books, and the younger Luke, with his sports. Amanda spent most of her time when she was at home, in the sitting room she meticulously decorated, with her friends or playing her moody pieces on the piano.

Neil saw himself as a simple man, the admiration of the good things in life giving him all the satisfaction he needed. His life had turned out exactly the way it should have, with school honors, career achievements, and finally Professor after years of hard work, and then a good marriage and children. He was a satisfied man and but also a humble one and he was grateful for what he had. But he worried at times that this simpleness would not be enough to satisfy his younger wife.

At first it had confused him, the small changes in Amandas' behaviour, as he thought they'd been happy until now, and he'd seen no evidence to suggest otherwise; they were a normal couple, bringing up their children, looking after their ailing parents and continuing on with life.

Now suddenly, he had noticed a slight shift, a barely imperceptible change, in the way they communicated with each other, and today he had finally consciously recognised it as a fact, after Amandas' outburst.

Something was different with Amanda and it was affecting all of them. And he now realised it had been going on over the last year. Or perhaps the family was just growing and changing in the healthy way that it should be over time. He hoped this was the case, and until he found out otherwise there was no reason to overreact.

In hindsight he had expected it at some point, her reaction to the difference in age groups, her realising that he would become older much quicker than she would; but he'd forgotten about it, and actually thought they might have gotten away with it.

But he knew the boys were noticing things as well. Her being constantly distracted from their lives, disengaged, not really paying attention to what was being said. He always wished they'd had a girl as well, a closer companion of her own gender in the family, he thought would have grounded her more, but when he suggested they have another child, she dismissed the idea, joking that they'd be elderly parents. She was very close to Luke anyway, he would always be the baby of the family.

They'd all become too detached from each others lives, that was the trouble. They were all doing different things at different times, not doing anything together as a family anymore, and until now it hadn't mattered. But now it was noticeable. It was his fault, he should have noticed it sooner. He would suggest they spend some time together. Perhaps they could all find some time to go on a holiday, before the boys got too much older and began their own lives and families.

He hoped it wasn't too late, but eternally the optimist, he would never have believed that anyway.

It started in the morning at breakfast. Amanda seemed irritated, and preoccupied.
"Are you alright Mandy?" Neil leaned in to kiss her on the cheek but she pulled away. He used his pet name for her, but

he never realised that she didn't really like it.

"Why do you have to call me that?!" she answered in disgust and moved away, continuing whatever she was doing with the toast and marmalade.

"I'm sorry darling." He moved towards the large pine kitchen table and sat down. He thought she must be embarrassed with the boys in the room. He began reading his paper.

Amanda looked at him and seethed inwardly. He doesn't care when he upsets me she thought. Then she placed both her hands on the bench and looked out the window at the beautifully manicured lawn around the pool fence. She wished just once Neil would let the grass grow wild, but it never crossed his mind. She breathed a huge sigh and knew she was being unfair. He was such a good husband and father, she couldn't have found better. The problem was with her not him. She leant down and kissed his cheek, and he smiled without looking up. This annoyed her again, sometimes she felt like she was one of his children, or one of his students, being rewarded for good behaviour.

Then the toast popped and she saw the marmalade. The sight of that marmalade that she'd spread on her husbands toast for twenty years tipped her over the edge.

She picked up the plate and the marmalade jar, walked over to the table and slammed them both down in front of him.

"Couldn't you just once try something else for a change!" She stared at him with anger and he looked up at her in surprise.

"Something else?" He looked genuinely bewildered.

"Strawberry or raspberry or honey! Why not honey, just once!"

"Leave him alone, mum."

"Oh so you want to weigh in on this too? Would it be too much to ask just for you all to try something different for a change? Just once?" Amanda looked at her older son with hidden pride, he was just like his father.

"We like marmalade don't we Dad?", he smiled conciliatory at his father.

Neil got up and put his arm around his wife's shoulders. "She's

just a bit stressed, that's all. Why don't you stay home today, love, do something for yourself?" He smiled at her as if he was comforting one of the boys after they'd been grazed at soccer.
"Ohh!" She shrugged off his arm and hurried out of the room and up the stairs.
"You're always defending her Dad, sometimes she's downright mean!"
"I know, but she's not herself lately. Don't worry, I'll talk to her later tonight."
"See you later Dad!"
"Bye son."
But Neil knew he wouldn't. He knew she wasn't opening up to him at the moment and he'd just have to let her ride it out.
    Upstairs in her bathroom Amanda burst into tears at how she had spoken to her son. She shook her head and looked at her swollen eyes in the mirror. She turned on the tap and watched the water running forcefully down and into the drain.
    Then she washed her face and got ready for work.

FRANK AND ROSIE

The first time Frank met Rosie was when he was eleven years old. His father had died of a heart attack that year, most likely brought on by his excessive drinking habit, and Frank had been sent to live with his only relatives in the country, his uncle and six cousins. They lived in Logan Heights as well, only two blocks away, but he would disappear every time his father said he was going to visit his brother, Frank's uncle. He hated his cousins, they always picked on him and beat him up, and now he had to go and live with them. His life was hell with his father and it would be the same with his uncle. Maybe worse. But he had no choice, as his mother was in and out of hospital and could not take care of him.

His cousins had not taken favourably to him entering their family home. He didn't talk or interact much and so was seen as a kind of simpleton, but that was mostly because he was timid from being belted by his father every day since he could remember. His father, while he was alive, made it his mission to let Frank know that he was worth nothing and would never amount to anything in his whole life, and Frank took it to heart. It made him shy, reserved and self conscious around others, and because of that he got picked on. He wasn't stupid, he just had his thinking beaten out of him.

Today was a regular day at his cousins house. He woke to find they had played some trick on him as usual, like cracking an egg on his pillow while he slept or putting water in his bed and then telling his uncle he weed the bed again. Today they had found a new trick. He woke to find obscene words written on his face. He tried his hardest to scrub it off but he knew he would be late for breakfast and would be in trouble again.

His cousins were relentlessss and they picked on him on the way to school. By the time they arrived he was getting angry, and when one of them poured some water down his back he lashed out and the fighting started.
"Stop it!" Down in the scrum Frank heard a girls voice.
"Stop it you bullies! Leave Frank alone!"

Rosie was an only child, unusual in a Mexican household, and lived next door to his uncle's house. She was the apple of her father's eye and he doted on her. If you crossed Rosie, you crossed her father, and that was a big mistake. Her father worked in an office and his family were one of the rare ones in the neighbourhood that had come across the border legally. But he wore his tradition proudly and was an advocate of the Mexican community. Frank's uncle hardly ever saw eye to eye with him but he was a respected figure, and respect was everything.

So when Rosie spoke, Frank's cousins listened.
She pushed them aside and took Frank's arm.
She pulled him up carefully. "Are you alright?" she asked him.
"Ye, ye I'm ok", he couldn't help a wry smile.
She turned to his cousins and poked them one by one, and said very slowly, "Leave him alone!"
Then the bell went. But Frank had never had a better day his whole life.

Rosie became the love of Franks life. She was

everything to him and more. She was the only thing that was even remotely connecting him with this Earth apart from his mother. She was the only thing that represented normality in his world because everything else was fraught with pain, the pain of his childhood, the pain of his non-existent family, the pain of being part of a gang, the pain of work, where he had to keep his temper under control or he would lose his job, and the pain of knowing that one day he would lose his beloved mother, the last connection he had with anyone or anything. She was the only thing that kept him sane. And because he loved and needed her so much, he held on too tightly.

They were unofficial childhood sweethearts and had known each other since they were toddlers. As Rosie grew older she didn't flirt with the tough guys of the gang like the other girls, and soon it became known that she was Franks girl. And it wasn't long before everyone knew that if you messed with Rosie, you were a dead man.

It was finally cemented when Rosie turned 15. Ricky was Franks cousin of the same age, but that was the only thing they had in common. Ricky had all the good looks and the charm to go with it, everything it seemed, that Frank lacked. And Ricky hated Frank. Frank had grown up with Ricky and Ricky's papa hated Frank as much as he was proud of his youngest son. He resented having to take on Frank after his father died when he had enough kids of his own to raise. And Ricky followed his fathers lead. He never missed the opportunity to bully Frank or get him in trouble, and Frank had to silently bear the punishment, for if he were to injure one of his cousins, his uncle would have killed him.

But one day Ricky crossed the line. Rosie was turning fifteen and it was a big deal. She was looking forward to her Quinceanera, and her and her friends couldn't stop talking about it, and planning what she was going to wear, approved by her mother and aunties, of course. Rosie's parents were throwing a huge party for their only daughter turning fifteen, and the whole neighbourhood was invited.

The day began with the family and close friends attending catholic mass. Rosie looked like a princess dressed in a flamboyant frilled white dress, a full tulle skirt spreading out from her slim waist.

She seemed to have suddenly grown up in the eyes of all the boys and they were in awe. They fumbled around her and said stupid things but she ignored them; she always had a soft spot for Frank. She saw something in him that no one else could. When she looked in his eyes she saw a sensitivity that the other boys lacked, and she was the only one who could draw him into conversation. They spent long hours talking alone and they were always sitting on her front porch every day after school; it was the only place Frank felt safe from his cousin's torment, and it earned him a begrudging respect in everyone's eyes. Rosie's mother and father were the only adults that spoke to him without harshness or brutality.

During the ceremony Rosie was awarded a gold locket by Franks auntie and uncle, and a sparkling tiara by her family, which made her look like an angel. After the mass, Rosie's parents invited everyone over to their house for a formal reception, where Rosie chose Frank to be her dancing partner. Everyone admired the couple as they danced around the families big lounge room, but Frank's cousin Ricky was seething. He could hardly contain his jealousy and he paced angrily around the room. But no one noticed him , and Frank and Rosie danced and laughed as if they had no cares in the world, and when they looked in each others eyes they knew they were in love. Everyone could see it.

Afterwards there was a huge cake, a special traditional one called tres leeches, and lots of food, more food than Frank had ever seen in his life, and lots of relatives and friends of Rosie"s family. The party went all night and in the wee hours of the morning it spilled onto the street. The teenagers had stolen some alcohol from the adults and they were sharing it around.

Frank and Rosie were in a state of excitement after the events of the day and were chatting animatedly behind a bush in the front yard when Ricky sidled up intoxicated. "So the birthday girls hanging around losers again." Ricky moved closer as he spoke and Frank, who had been drinking as well, rose up to meet him. They stood for a minute glaring at each other before Rosie stepped between them.

"Shut up Ricky. What do you want?"

"I came to get my birthday kiss what else?" And with that he leered towards her.

Rosie shrank back and Frank pushed between them. He sneered into Ricky's face, hardly able to control his mounting anger. "Now that's something you're never going to get!" Frank was feeling unusually happy after the events of the day and felt an air of confidence he usually couldn't muster.

"Oh yeah, and who's gonna stop me?" Ricky now knew that Rosie would never be his and he was furious. He looked at Frank with all the hatred he had ever felt but this time there was something about Frank that looked different, a glimmer of strength, and that made him even angrier.

"Who do you think?" Frank moved towards Ricky causing

him to stumble back, but he collected himself and came
back.

"You wouldn't dare."

Frank could smell the alcohol on Ricky's breath and so
knew that he was partly working from a senseless place
but when it came to Rosie there was no defence.

"Please Ricky, go away, leave us alone!" Rosie knew that
this time Frank would not back down and she was scared.
She really didn't want anyone to get hurt or cause trouble
on her special day.

"You're spoiling my day Ricky, get lost!" With this she
shoved him but he didn't move.

"Oh really. I thought hanging around losers would spoil it
more. Why don't you come with me for a ride?" Ricky
didn't have his licence but that didn't stop him driving
when he could find a car. It was common for all of them to
steal cars, drive them for a while before dumping them
somewhere or burning them, and then get another one.

"No thanks." Rosie took Frank's hand and started to walk
away, but Ricky grabbed her arm. If there was one thing
Ricky could not take, it was rejection by a girl, and
especially publicly, the way Rosie had done today; and
especially not for Frank.

"You're coming with me!" He said pulling on her arm.

"Let go of me!" Rosie pulled her arm away. "Leave me
alone!"

If there was one thing Frank would not stand for it was the
sound of Rosie in distress. He heard her cry out and his
blood began to boil.

   He lunged at Ricky and punched him square in the face.
Ricky fell back onto the lawn, blood coming from his
nostrils. He got up and flung a punch at Frank but Frank
was too quick and downed him again. All the times he had

taken a beating because of Ricky and put up with his bullying now came to the fore and he was not holding back. He jumped on him and started pelting his face, the pent up rage a force not to be reckoned with.

At the back of his mind he could hear Rosie's yelling, but he didn't comprehend anything in his fury. The commotion attracted attention and it took three of Ricky's brothers to drag Frank off him.

"What the hell's going on?!" The older brother Carlos took charge.

"It was Ricky's fault, he wouldn't leave me alone!" Rosie came to Frank's defence. "Let him go!" She pulled Frank away from his cousins.

"And then he attacked Frank!" Although Frank knew now that Rosie loved him, he was still surprised that she would go to such lengths for him.

"You're gonna be in trouble when Dad finds out Ricky. He doesn't want any trouble here today." Carlos knew how obnoxious his youngest brother could be. "You better lay low for a while." He nodded in the direction of the house. "Go!"

Frank and Rosie quickly moved off and disappeared together into the night. After that they were inseparable. Ricky was out of action for a couple of weeks and after that steered clear of Rosie forever. To his great surprise no one talked about the incident again, and no one ever even looked at Rosie in that way again. Frank had let everyone know what would happen if they did. It was the only time his family ever let him get away with anything. But it was enough.

THE ACTRESS

Amanda had had a difficult day at work. Two residents had passed that week and today she'd had to fill out the final release details for them. The job was a tedious one, and filling out the final details for a person lent itself to too much reflection. She usually coped pretty well with the emotional fallout, it was part of her job, but lately she'd been thinking is this all that it's about? She couldn't help thinking that it wouldn't be that long till it was her wheeled out on the trolley with the sheet over her head.

She knew it was crazy to think that way, she wasn't even fifty yet. But she couldn't shake the dread and fear she felt about growing older. She should be looking forward to the boys' becoming independent and her and Neil growing old together, retiring from work, and going on holidays. She also couldn't shake the feeling that everything was so pointless. The struggles of being a child and growing up, trying so hard to find your identity, to "succeed" in your chosen profession, to mature, have children, then grow old and die, only for your children and their children to do it all over again.

The saddest thing of all was that she had no one she could talk to about these things. Everyone was so busy living; she didn't want to worry them with her irrational thoughts and she didn't want to be labelled as depressed or not well. Whenever someone was labelled they became the subject of concern and needed 'care'. She did not want to be seen like that and she did not want to burden her family.

So she continued on with her family and her work, as if nothing was wrong.

But there was.

Increasingly she was feeling alone and isolated, separated from the ones that she should have been feeling close to. She knew Neil would not understand; he was the eternal optimist always thinking everything had a quick fix. She wished it was true. She hated the way she felt, she wished she could stop being so negative all the time, about everything, but she looked at everything as if it was covered by a grey cloud, a cloud that swirled around her, sometimes dark like a thunderstorm, sometimes light like a big ball of grey fluff, reaching out in front of her and touching everything she saw. It never cleared, it was always there, looking over her shoulder, tainting every thought, every emotion.

She didn't tell anyone, but she had begun to have panic attacks. They would start suddenly, without any warning, and she would be engulfed in a horrible feeling of needing to run, run away from wherever she was or whatever she was doing; and then she couldn't breathe, she was choking, and if she was standing she would fall over if she didn't steady herself.

If she was at work she'd run to a quiet room or the public toilets. If she was at home she'd lock herself in her bathroom. Sometimes during an attack it would be so bad that she became nauseous and vomited. These attacks made her feel worse about her depression, she began to revile herself and her perceived weakness of becoming sick, and after a while her self loathing consumed her to the point where she hated looking in the mirror. It also made her more determined than ever to keep the way she was feeling a secret.

Amanda became an expert actress. Her colleagues could not tell there was anything wrong, she was deliberately chatty and bright. She'd open up her eyes and smile widely when someone spoke to her and spoke in length to her lonely patients, asking them about their family and interests, books they'd read or the latest movie they'd watched. The patients and her co workers always found her to be bright and cheerful, and actually thought that lately she was happier than ever. To her patients she was caring and attentive, a smiling face always ready to listen; and to her co workers she was the consummate professional, reliable, dependable, cheerful.

Little did they know how wrong they all were. They did not seem to notice that she was notably absent from the staff room during breaks; that she spent a lot of time in the ladies room alone; or that she never attended staff functions or get togethers; that lately she was becoming more reserved when talking about her private life and that she was not pursuing friendships at work.

Her family had no idea either. They didn't see each other much really anyway, her and Neil were working, the boys were at school or playing sport or hanging with their friends, and lately they didn't always have dinner together. It was something they'd always insisted on when the boys were younger but now it was a bit unreasonable with all of them having so much on. When they did see each other Amanda had become an expert in diverting attention away from herself, encouraging the boys' to elaborate their stories of their daily experiences, so as not to have to talk about herself; and as for Neil she just tried to avoid him altogether.

As a trained nurse she knew that she was living all the signs of depression, and she accepted that she suffered from it, but within herself she felt that she was justified in being depressed. She knew it was a condition that made everything seem hopeless, but she really believed everything was hopeless in her life. Her parents had not been pleased with her for reasons of their own, not necessarily anything to do with her, they had their own unresolved issues, but she felt permanently affected by their unhealthy behaviour. As far as her marriage was concerned, she thought perhaps her mother had been right when she said that Neil may be too old for her. He had never had the spark she enjoyed with earlier boyfriends and she always wondered if she'd done the right thing marrying him. Did she do it just to be seen as more mature or perhaps she liked him because he was older and different to the guys her own age? This reel ran over and over in her mind and she really did not want to know the answer to these questions. And she knew that Neil would be horrified and hurt if he knew what she was really thinking.

As for her future it looked bleak. The boys would grow older and leave and she would grow older with Neil.

She wanted something more, she needed something more.

She just didn't know what that something was. But what she did know was that things could not go on the way they were. Something had to happen; and it would.

HER BAD MOOD

Amanda was in a bad mood. It seemed everything was going wrong today; she was nearly late because of a train delay, she'd left home without her prepared lunch, and she wasn't looking forward to having dinner with Neil's friends tonight after work. Her patients seemed to be more demanding than usual and to make things worse she was reminded that she had a meeting with the head nurse straight after lunch, which meant she would have to eat canteen food instead of being able to go out and buy lunch so she would be exactly on time. The head nurse did not take kindly to tardiness. She hated eating on the run, and hated buying overpriced, sad sandwiches, or lukewarm heated junk food.

Yes, she could feel herself slipping into depression again these days and she was trying to stop it but at times she just succumbed and became annoyed as well. She could tell when depression was trying to take a hold on her and she knew that she was feeling it now. The truth was that she really did feel depressed. She felt unhappy about her life but because she knew she had a fortunate life compared to a lot of people, the feeling was filtered and compounded by guilt over her negative thinking. She saw herself as both selfish and childish to have these thoughts and therefore would not share them with anyone. She was feeling disassociated with her family and friends who were always asking her if anything was wrong, was she ok; what did they expect her to say? Did they really want to know that she was feeling unsatisfied and dislocated from her life? Did Neil really want to know that she couldn't stand to be in the same room with him anymore, let alone in the same bed? Did her friends really want to know that she saw them as petty and spoilt? That she felt she had nothing in common with them anymore? Did her colleagues want to know that she was sick of the sick being sick and that everything was not going to be just fine? She doubted it, no she knew it. If the people in her life knew what she was really thinking, they would be hurt and confused, and she did not want to deal with that. At the moment she had a negative view about everything in her life, and she couldn't shake it.

By the end of the day the cloud hanging over her head was a dark one and she knew she did not want to go to the dinner with friends that Neild had arranged for them. The last thing she wanted was feigned chatter over old times so she called Neil complaining of a migraine and elaborating apologies about dinner. He was understanding and she breathed a huge sigh of relief. She finished her shift and started the short walk to the train station. There was a park on the way and she often decided to stop and sit for a while before she started the journey home. She just needed some quiet, some time to herself to try to work out what was so wrong in her head. She walked over slowly to her favourite bench and sat down. She watched the pigeons picking at some unseen specks of food on the pavement near the road, and the Jay bird fussing in the large Oak tree overhead. Life was so simple for birds, no work, no house to keep spotless, no washing, no cooking all the time, flying around wherever you wanted to, and their lively chatter proved it. 'You're so lucky', she thought and sighed to herself.

One of the pastimes that Amanda did like to do was to stare at passersby.
She would study each one intensely, first their face but only briefly, then she would move to their clothes, their overall dress, to gain a total impression of them; but what really fascinated her was their mannerisms, the way they moved in the world. She would instantly ascertain whether they were cool and confident, young and immature, down and defeated, old and past it, or whatever. She could sit there and watch people for hours if she only had the time. She just wanted a

touch of reality, to feel a common bond, to try and work out that she was not the only person struggling in this world.

She watched a businessman walk briskly by in a black suit with a crimson tie; she saw a young woman jog by in her tights and colourful trainers; and she watched an even younger woman push a toddler in a stroller towards the swings. It was a typical scene in a park. Life repeated itself over and over again, but what was it like to be these other people. She'd love to swap lives with some of them, even for just a short time, but then again, she wouldn't wish her life on anyone. She guessed they felt the same as she did on various days, at various times. Sad, happy, loved, loving, annoyed, angry. The common emotions.

But her problem was that lately she felt that way all the time. She did not like her life and she did not want to be herself anymore. She felt empty and unfulfilled but didn't know what to do about it. The thought of never having lived up to her father's expectations preyed on her mind; she felt like a failure a lot of the time.

Increasingly she also felt guilty that she was now failing her family, that she was not fulfilling the roles of wife and mother and being happy about it like she should be. at times these feelings weighed on her mind so badly that she was beside herself, and she had panic attacks. Her family didn't know it but she felt totally disconnected from them. It wasn't their fault, it was her fault. There was something wrong with her and sometimes she felt she was going mad. She didn't want to keep secrets about it either but she didn't want trouble in her life and she didn't want to burden them. She'd be fine in a while.

She knew she had to control her over-emotional thinking and became adept at snapping over into a practical 'mode'. It made it possible to block out her bad feelings for a while, and she was then able to function and do her duties, at work and at home. That was her way of coping, to switch off.

She watched two women walk by who were covered from head to toe with the Muslim burkah. They were chattering to each other animatedly, not seeming to realise that there were many people in this society who looked on them as being suppressed. In her eyes of course, as a Christian American born woman, this is what immediately popped into Amanda's mind. It always fascinated her when she saw these women, just getting on with their lives as if they're behaviour was not unusual, which indeed it was not to them, but it certainly was questionable to a woman such as herself.

She wanted to rip off their coverings and say "Go! Run! Do it now! Be free!", and she wondered why they never did that. On a whim she got up from the seat and decided to follow them. She would follow them and try to work out why they did not run away from their, what seemed to Amanda must be, restricted and limiting lives.

It had been a couple of months since she donned the full covering of the burkah and had met Aleyah in the city, and that experience had taught her that she could not be disrespectful to these women by doing that again, but she still felt fascinated by their mysterious lives. And because she was bored with her own life and stressed about her depression, she acted again upon her impulses, something she may not have done if she was not in a strange place with herself.

The women walked to the edge of the park and down the road to the bus stop and as Amanda followed them, she did not keep her distance or hide her presence, after all there was no reason that they would think they were being followed. The women stood talking animatedly and Amanda sat down on the bus stop seat near them. It was a simple plastic seat and she couldn't help wondering why the City insisted on making them as an uncomfortable chair as she'd ever sat on. They were of different ages, the two women, one being a young woman perhaps in her twenties, and the other a lot older, probably around the same age as Amanda was. They spoke mainly in their foreign tongue, a bit of English mixed in, and so Amanda could not really get the gist of what they were saying.

Amanda sat a couple of seats away from the two women in the bus, mainly because she couldn't understand what they were saying anyway and also because she didn't want them to notice her at all.

The two Muslim women alighted from the bus and began walking along Balboa Avenue. Amanda got off the bus and decided to put a bit of distance between herself and the women, after all she had no problem seeing where they were going on this long stretch of road. She started to feel a bit self counscious about what she was doing but decided there was no harm in it and she could change her mind and turn around at any time.

But she wanted to get out of the ordinary for a while and walking in this unfamiliar neighborhood was just what she needed to clear her mind for a while. She walked slowly and the distance between herself and the women became longer, but she could still see them in the distance. It was a lovely sunny day and she was enjoying her meandering and the warmth on her back.

The street was busy with lots of cars zooming past her and people everywhere coming in and out of the shops and businesses. All the people were busy, busy, busy like ants, and for once she wasn't one of them. She felt a hint of joy at doing something different than the daily routine, and consciously smile at herself. She thought she was perhaps being a bit childish but she enjoyed the feeling anyway.

After what seemed like a long time the two women in the distance turned into left and so Amanda quickened her steps so that she could see where they went.

She caught up to where she'd seen them turn and go out of sight. Of course, this is where they were going. She was standing in front of the Islamic Centre of San Diego. She went and sat on a seat in the front of the imposing blue and white building just watching the people go in and out. It was a school but most of the children had already left but there were still people coming and going. She sat in the sun again enjoying her relaxation and closed her eyes to the warmth.

"Excuse me! Are you here for the class?"

Amanda was startled. "Sorry?"

"I was just wondering, are you here for the class. It's about to start."

In front of her stood a women in a burkah, but with her face open.

Amanda was taken aback but she quickly composed herself and lied.

"Yes, yes I am here for the class," and she smiled at the woman.

"Well come in and I'll show you where to go."

Amanda couldn't believe her luck, now she would find out exactly how these women lived. Yes she'd take a class, that would be the perfect way to try and work out what their lives were like.

"My name is Fatimah, I'll be one of the women taking the class. I hope you enjoy it. Do you know much about Islam?"

"No, nothing really."

"Well you've come to the right place then, welcome."

Fatimah's eyes were warm and she smiled back at Amanda.

"Thank you." Amanda got up and followed Fatimah out of the warm sunshine and into the esoteric, intriguing building.

AMANDA'S MUM

A strange thing was happening. It was so odd that Amanda
felt confused and ashamed at the same time.

Amanda was a religious woman. No one really knew how
seriously she took her religious beliefs except for her. She
would regularly attend the local Baptist church every Sunday
even after her husband and her children lost interest and
decided not to attend any more.

Every Sunday morning she would begin the ritual of driving
to her mothers house, prepare their breakfast, and then drive
her mother to church. They would sit in the same seats every
week and listen to the slow monotone of the aging pastor.
After a little while Amanda's mind would begin to wander,
about all kinds of different things, and then jolt back to the
present, and then wander again throughout the whole sermon.
At the end her mother would then sit and have tea in the small
back timber room with ladies the same sort of age as herself,
while Amanda would spend ten minutes in the prayer room
down on her knees and then walk out and sit on the old
chipped, blue painted garden seat under the large ficus in the
small backyard behind the church building. At the end of
winter she would close her eyes and feel the soft touch of the
furry pink blossoms fall down on her shoulders; and in the
summer she would collect the small red fruit and pop them in
her mouth, sucking out the juice before spitting out the pip
onto the gravel pathway. She felt that wasn't very ladylike,
especially at church, but it made her feel young and naughty.
It was so long since she had felt anything like that.

It was at these times that she would spend thinking about her
life and how it had turned out and praying that God would be
good to her. It was at these times that she felt closest to God

and that she could release the paralyzing despair she held in her heart. It was no ones fault, not her parents nor her husbands, or her own, she knew, but she just thought that her life would have been different. She wasn't even sure what that life would have looked like, especially since she felt quite satisfied with her work as a nurse looking after the elderly, it was immensely rewarding and a lot of the time humbling, but she felt there was an emptiness inside her, an unanswered question, and she felt it deep within her; it was like an ache in her stomach that she couldn't get rid of.

And now as she was spending more time with the deeply religious Muslim ladies she met in town, she felt her own religion taking on a deeper meaning. She was beginning to identify with them in some strange way and after her trips to their meetings she was becoming reluctant to take her headscarf off after each visit. She'd discarded the uncomfortable burka after only wearing it a couple of times, and now wore a simple headdress to cover her head during her visits to the Muslim mosque and the Muslim communities.

She didn't understand this about herself but she believed that the head scarf was associated with respecting God when in His presence, and increasingly she felt like she was in His presence rather than just functioning in her roles as nurse, wife and mother. So she would now leave it on until the last minute before she walked through her door at home. She would wear it on the train home and leave it on as she walked through her quiet suburb in the dusk. She would pull it off her hair wistfully as she rounded the corner of her street, and tuck it into her bag ready for the next day. At times she thought it might be the rebel in her just enjoying extending her little secret to the maximum, but she knew the reason that she continued visiting her new friends was something more. And inexplicable though this behaviour may have been, she went along with it. All part of her little project, not harming anyone, she told herself every time she could not explain to herself what she was doing. It was always the last rationale, the last retreat from plausible reason. Anyway, she sometimes thought, her need for explanation was only to satisfy the lack of understanding that her family would have if they ever discovered what she was doing in her spare time, and that was unlikely. But she resented that she might have to explain at all, even if she had no explanation herself, and she didn't want to dwell on her reasons, whatever they may be in her unsatisfied subconscious.

Amanda felt the comforting warmth of the morning sun on her face as the golden rays filtered through the bare branches of the old cherry tree in the back of the older church. But she knew she had to get up and take her mother home. Her mother was not well and it showed in her downcast moods and ailing thin frame. But Amanda could do no more for her than what she was already doing, and found that being in her mothers company depressed her. She dreaded picking her up in the morning to take her to church or the doctor or the hospital, or the pharmacy, and yearned for the day to end after she'd completed these mundane but necessary chores for her mother. She felt guilty about these thoughts but they were a natural reaction and ones that she tried her best to put out of her mind and do her duty.

She tried many times to form a deeper relationship with her failing mother, but they could never quite sew together the great divide that separated them from eachother. Amanda felt this was a great flaw in her personality and took the blame upon herself as her mother seemed always open and affable these days, but in her darkest moments of self analysis, Amanda felt that she was losing the ability to love anyone at all, losing all the connections with the people she held most dear. At times she thought maybe she should get some counselling but then she'd discard the thought, and tuck her worries away somewhere in the recycling bin of her mind and forget about them. She'd get them out one day and muse over them then.

And with her work, her mum, her family, and her extra activities, forgetting, ignoring, avoiding her inner turmoil, was easy to do.

AMANDA AND FATIMAH

Amanda had begun attending regular classes at the Muslim centre. She'd started learning about the Muslim faith and though uncommital she found it interesting. She was also getting to know Fatimah and the other women who attended the mosque every day and they welcomed her into their midst.

Amanda found them to be very different from any of the other women she'd ever met in her life. They had a closeness that was more than just friendship, they seemed to genuinely care for each other in an active way. They had a ritualistic life in that their days were centred around their prayer times at the temple, these were and so they were in each other's company for long hours each day. But instead of finding this stifling they had formed a supportive bond with each other, and it was their lifeline.

Fatimah and the other ladies were at the temple every day, they either worked there or volunteered there, or just visited on a regular basis as part of their family prayer times, or just because they had nothing else to do.

Amanda had a class on Wednesday evening learning about becoming a Muslim and another on Sunday afternoon learning about the Koran, the Muslim's version of the Christian Bible. She had mixed feelings about attending the classes, as she really had no real intention to convert to Muslim, but she enjoyed the closeness she immediately felt with the women she met, and she felt that instead of making her feel less like a Christian, she actually was feeling more spiritual than she ever had.

When she prayed with the Muslim women it was so different to praying at the stifling Christian church she attended with her mother. The prayer times were the most important part of the day at the temple and Amanda found it quiet and beautiful, to sit on a mat with all the other women and bow down to her Lord unashamedly. At the church only a few young people prayed in this way and that was in a small private, cold back room and Amanda would have felt ridiculed and embarrassed to go in there.

It had been a long time since somebody had looked after Amanda, and Fatimah seemed to have made it her mission to do so. She seemed to be at Amanda's side all the time, and over the weeks and months they had many discussions about life, religion, family and anything else that came up in conversation, and their views were not that different.

One day there was the sound of arguing in the entrance way of the temple and Fatimah, being a senior teacher in the temple, rushed out to see what the commotion was. Amanda followed, interested to see who might be arguing in such a holy place, as it was unusual.

When they got to the scene of the fracas, they found a man holding the arm of a teenage girl, while she squirmed and tussled to try to pull away from him.

"What is going on here, Marsad?" Fatimah directed her question at the man holding the young girl and she seemed to know him.

Immediately he let go and spoke to the girl in a gruff voice. "Greet your teacher Nashida." He then turned to Fatima. "As sala'amu alaikum Fatima."

Fatima replied, "As sala'amu alaikum wa rahmatullahi."

Nashida also greeted Fatima with an obligatory look, " As sala'amu alaikum."

Fatima replied, " As sala'amu alaikum wa rahmatullahi."

Marsad then began to explain. 'Nashida was leaving without my permission. She has not finished her studies and wants to go out with her friends. She is spending too much time with her friends and does not want to come to the temple anymore. Can you help Fatima?" His eyes held the look of a man in despair.

"May I suggest some counsel with both of you separately Marsad? It can be hard for young people born in this country to try and merge the two lifestyles of Muslim and American. I know it will help both of you to understand better the influences affecting each others behaviour. There are also classes for parents and families dealing with children who are growing up in a non Muslim country. Perhaps you would consider attending them?"

"Thank you, I will consider it." Marsad turned to his daughter. "You will speak with Fatima, and then I will see you at home." He then turned and walked inside.

"Come Nashida, we will go and sit in the women's chambers. This is Amanda, she is learning about the Muslim faith."

  The female area of the temple was a plush one. With beautiful long drapes adorning the high windows and comfortable couches of what seemed like velvet and lush colours of gold and green and subtle orange, it was a joy to spend time in.

The woman spent long hours eating and discussing different topics and this is where Fatimah and Amanda brought Nashida.

"Oh, it's beautiful in here!" she exclaimed. "I've never been in here before." When Nashida smiled she looked lovely with her bright, dark eyes, and flowing auburn hair. Amanda knew she must be having a hard time resisting the boys that were undoubtedly chasing her. She hoped her father was not too unreasonable.

"Sit down here, my dear, I'll get you something to eat and some tea."

Amanda was left sitting with Nashida and began a conversation.

"How old are you Nashida?"

"I'm sixteen but my father treats me like I was ten!"

"It must be hard for him watching you grow up so fast, he's only trying to protect you."

  Amanda never had any attention from her father when she

was growing up, she could hardly remember speaking to him at all, and he never knew where she was or what she was doing, he just wasn't interested, and though she knew that the attention Nashida was getting from her father may seem a bit over protective, she wished her own father would have had an interest in her. She decided to share this with Nashida.

"You know when I was growing up my father didn't care where I was or what I was doing. I was hardly ever home and because of that I did some things that I now regret. I had a lot of freedom Nashida and now I wish I'd had someone who cared about me enough to keep me out of trouble and guide me a little bit. You're so lucky to have that."

Nashida at first pulled a rebellious face, but as Amanda spoke about her own family she seemed to be considering it and was quietly listening.

"Yes, I guess I see what you're saying, but I really would like a bit more freedom."

"To do what exactly?"

"Well my friends from school don't have to be home at a certain time on the weekend, and they can have a boyfriend."

"Don't you think you're too young to have a boyfriend? You should be concentrating on your studies and where you want your future to be, your career."

"You sound just like my parents."

"Maybe they want what is best for you. You know when you have a boyfriend they take your mind off your studies and onto them. They can be very distracting and can get you into a lot of trouble with your family. I think you should try to wait until you finish your schooling then think about boys. What are you studying?"

"I am studying science, maths and biology, I want to be a doctor." She smiled triumphantly as if she'd already achieved her plans.

"That's wonderful, you know I'm a nurse." Amanda was glad they had something in common.

Fatima arrived with the tea and started pouring. She had some older girls with her and introduced them.

"Nashida, Amanda, this is Elisha and Samia."

They looked just a little older than Nashida and Amanda guessed what Fatima was doing.

"Sit down girls, get to know each other. Elisha goes to your high school Nashida, she thought you might want to do some things together. What are you doing this weekend Elisha?"

"We're going to the movies and then we're going to a Muslim coffee shop around the corner. Would you like to come Nashida?"

"Yeah sure, that would be great, thanks."

"That's settled then." Fatimah smiled self assuredly. "I've spoken to your father, he said it's fine, and the girls will bring you home before eleven."

"Eleven, wow, he's never let me out that late before, thanks Mudarris^."

"I said *before* eleven," she laughed and gave the girl a big hug.

The women and girls sat around talking for a while and then it was time for everyone to head home at the end of the day. Fatimah and Amanda stayed a while longer and sat talking until they too headed home.

On the way home Amanda wondered at the close ties she felt with these Muslim women, and the wonderful feeling of faith in God that she had come to after worshipping so openly and honestly at the mosque over the last few months. Her spiritual faith had grown and her belief in other people had grown also, as she spent more time with Fatimah. She thought she'd lost both of these things and she felt a faint stirring of love and happiness as she arrived home.

^teacher.

DAVID ALVAREZ

_David Alvarez was born in San Diego to Jose and Maria Alvarez and had four brothers and one sister. He grew up in Barrio Logan and attended the local public schools: Perkins Elementary, Memorial Junior High, and then San Diego High School. He was the first in his family to graduate from high school and college and he graduated with honors from San Diego State University.

He began his career as a social services worker and after-school teacher. Soon after he was selected to the prestigious Capitol Fellows Program where he served under the Secretary of State. After his return to San Diego, he worked with a company that develops new opportunities for affordable housing and later represented the State Senator as a community liaison. He was elected to the City Council, defeating Felipe Hueso with sixty percent of the vote. He had roles of Chair of the Natural Resources & Culture Committee, Vice Chair of the Land Use & Housing Committee, and a member of the Budget & Finance and Rules & Economic Development Committees.

Additionally, he served on the San Diego Regional County Airport Authority, San Diego Metropolitan Transit System Board, SANDAG Borders Committee, Otay Valley Regional Park Policy Committee, Bayshore Bikeway Working Group, and the San Diego Consortium Policy Board. He also served on the Board of Director's for Local Progress, a national municipal policy network.

It was obvious that David was ambitious and bold, especially in view of his background and upbringing. It was the realisation that his mother and his family lived in abject poverty and in a dismal, noxious environment that spurred him into a career of political change. It was inevitable that he would pursue his intention for Mayor in the neighborhood where he grew up, and he declared his candidacy for Mayor of San Diego. He was only thirty three years old. He was the officially endorsed Democratic candidate in the special election to replace Bob Filner and in the primary election held, he came in second with twenty five percent of the vote. In the runoff election against fellow city council member Kevin Faulconeras he was defeated but remained a councillor for many years.

Rosie's father was active in the Mexican community of San Diego and therefore he earned a respect that was rare in his world. His goal was to make Logan Heights a better place to live. He had friends in high places but because he was against drugs and violence he was always on the wrong side of the gangs who controlled the area and the drug trade between Tijuana, on the Mexican side of the border, and San Diego.

The gangs and the Cartels knew him well, especially because he had ties with the police and the Feds in the US, and while usually he would have been a target, because he was demonstrative for the Mexican community at ground level and was intimately involved with the local families, he had managed some protection over the years.

He had gotten away with it by the skin of his teeth on many occasions, but he was determined to try and improve the living standards of the local families and show the kids that there was another way to live life rather than joining the gangs.

He would recruit ex gang members to give talks at the local schools, libraries or community centres, and he would make overtures to gang and cartel leaders to have discussions on ending the drug trade and making the area safer for families to live in. They would never agree to meet him but recognised his standing as a pillar of the community and his courage in approaching them.

The most important thing to David and his wife Xochitl, was his family and his only child Rosie. His wife had had two miscarriages and one sitllborn baby before Rosie arrived healthy one week before his fortieth birthday and the celebrations went on for days. She was a coveted child and she was doted on by all the relatives and friends of the family. Every birthday of hers was a huge affair with large dinners and many guests in their home, that was palatial by Barrio Logan standards.

But David would insist on inviting guests who were rich or poor, professional or not, to his celebrations; there was no inequality or discrimination where he was concerned. Everyone who had ever known Rosie or his family were invited, as long as they followed the rules when they walked into his house. No weapons, no drugs, no violence.

David's parties were grand affairs, and he never had a problem.

If there was one thing Mexican people held dear it was respect for the Church and the people who looked out for their families. David was one of these people. And although he was on the other side of the law compared to them, and could not be corrupted, the leaders of the gangs gave him a wide berth, knowing that although he was an upholder of the law, he grew up with them and understood their world.

As they grew older and went separate ways David had his clashes with the gang leaders in the area but they developed a mutual understanding of getting on with business and keeping out of each other's way.

But as the gangs of Logan Heights strengthened their connections with the Tijuana Cartel across the border, and new faces appeared in the neighborhood it was getting harder for David not to appear as the enemy. And over time the faces in the gangs that were familiar died off or went to jail and were replaced by others who did not share the same alliances.

The new gang leaders became ruthless and at times

indiscriminate about who they targeted. The drug trafficking and increasing number of murders became impossible to control by the authorities, and Barrio Logan became a dangerous place to live.

But for David it was business as usual. He'd worked hard for what he believed in and was not going to be intimidated by the changing violence of the gangs around him. He'd seen it all before, in his own home, with his own brothers. He'd decided to follow a different path and he would not be discouraged.

Frank and Rosie sat every day after school on the front porch of her house. Frank had long left school three years ago and after working in the shipyard with his uncle for a short time, he left because he easily earned more money from working for the gang. But at four o'clock every day, if the gang did not need him for a job at that time, he would be standing waiting in front of her house. She wasn't allowed to meet him anywhere else and he obeyed any rule her parents made just to see her. Anyway, it was the only place he was accepted as a person, not just another member of the gang employed to do a job, a hit or a drop.

Rosie's mother brought them a snack as usual, a plate of churros or some creamy croquetas. The two were in a world of their own and had no mind for anyone or anything else when they sat there chatting excitedly and laughing, touching each other when they could or stealing a long kiss. They had been seeing each other with the approval of Rosie's parents for a year and a half now, ever since Rosie's fiftteenth birthday and her Quinceanera.

Although her father and Frank's uncle didn't really have a lot in common, they tolerated each other, and David had a soft spot for Frank. He saw Frank as the typical Logan Heights gang recruit, and he was trying to talk him into going back to school. Of course he knew that his uncle wouldn't hear of it, he wanted Frank to pay his own way, but he also knew that he didn't care where Frank got the money, through working or from drug money. But David did care and especially if Frank wanted to keep seeing his daughter. He did not want Rosie involved with anyone in a gang, and so he was making it his mission to curb Frank's criminal behaviour.

He could do this with a clear conscience, because ,like all bad kids in the neighborhood, they hardly had a choice about joining the gang, and he knew this was true of Frank, knowing his cousin's vocations and the pressure this must have put on Frank.

Each day when he returned from work David would invite Frank inside for dinner and they spent many hours discussing his dubious future. Frank humoured him and listened to his ideas for him and not only enjoyed the discussions, the dinners the acceptance, but also the chance to spend more time near Rosie. But he knew he could never leave the gang, his cousins would kill him; he'd be a dead man.

Today was a day like any other. He'd finished his day with his cousins, hanging around waiting for instructions from the gang leaders. Today there had been none, so he was waiting early.

Rosie got off the bus at the end of the street, and began walking towards him. He leant a against a concrete post, smoking, admiring her curved body and legs with the white socks pulled up to her knees, and her coy smile when she saw him.

He saw the car skid around the corner before he heard the shots, a car filled with Vels *crips,* gangbangers from a rival gang, and he knew either himself, Rosie or both of them were the targets.

He yelled as he pulled his biscuit from under his shirt but it was too late, and as his yell was cut short with a bullet hitting his shoulder, and another searing through his chest, he heard sharp cracks, and then he saw Rosie 's head tilt to the side and she fell to the ground with her blood spraying out all

around her.
Before he lost consciousness he knew she was dead.

Frank woke to find David standing over him at the hospital sobbing.
"What happened Frank?!"
Frank heard the desperation in his voice and knew that he had no answer. He knew David would never forgive him and he knew he would never forgive himself.
Gone was the light that shone in both of their lives, their hope, their reason for living. It was the thing that bonded them together, the thing they loved more than anything else in the world, the focus, the epicentre, of their lives. It was their Rosie.
Rosie stood for so much for so many people in their community. The protege of a family that did well, was successful, was a beacon in Logan Heights, without resorting to unlawful activities to do so.
Theirs was the one family who stood out from the rest, seemingly untouched by the gang wars and the violence that dominated all around them. Now that was all gone. No longer would they be the light in a dark world. They too were now destroyed by the environment they lived in, and they would never recover.
Frank did not know what to say. He knew nothing could take away the excruciating pain that he himself was feeling.
"I'm sorry I couldn't save her, I tried.....", he choked on his own tears.
He never spoke to David again. There was nothing to say.

When Frank got out of hospital the funeral for Rosie had already been held but he wouldn't have gone anyway. He heard it was a big affair with many important people attending. But for him to be in the proximity of her lying lifeless in that box would have driven him beyond insane. As it was there was going to be hell to pay.

Instead he had something else in mind.

He gathered together his cousins and anyone else in the gang who wanted to come along. They found out exactly who the guys were who had killed Rosie and they hunted them down. It only took a week of searching and they came across them two neighborhoods away at a pool hall. Frank and the he Logan Heights gang members went in armed to the teeth and everyone in the hall didn't stand a chance. In all nine people were killed including three young girls. The place was closed down, the perpetrators never caught. The local police intelligence were informed it was a revenge killing associated with the Rosie Alvarez murder and the Logan Heights gang, but the killers fled across the border to Mexico and laid low for a few months. They were never arrested and no one was ever charged.

MEXICO

Neil and Amanda were arguing. Amanda was becoming quite heated and Neil could not remember a time when their disagreements had no compromising expectation at all.

Neil felt confused. Lately Amanda had been working a lot, even on Sundays and when he mentioned this she just brushed him off and said that at the nursing home they were short staffed at the moment. She also had made a remark that he was always at golf with his buddy's, and so she thought he hadn't even noticed. And she was right for quite a while.

But lately he had started to notice the slight changes in Amanda's behaviour, but that wasn't his focus at this time. He was right now concerned with her latest plan.

She had told him that she planned to go with a nurse's group volunteering once a week, every Saturday, across the border into Mexico. She had noticed flyers at work asking for volunteers all the time, and she figured into Mexico wasn't far, she could work for a few hours over there, and be back for dinner time.

But Neil did not like the idea at all. He was never unsupportive of any idea a member of his family may have, and Amanda certainly did not need his permission to do anything, but this was one activity that he did not think was safe at all. He tried to tell her that everyone knew what a dangerous place Mexico was, but she just replied that was why they needed medical staff so badly.

"So do you think that the risk is of putting your life in danger to help those people is fair to your family? I'm not trying to make you feel guilty but I really do not believe it is fair on us, especially the boys. They need you, if anything were to happen to you they'd be devstated."

"I understand that Neil, but actually they don't need me at all. They're both so independent now, we hardly ever see them, and that's the point, these people do need more qualified nurses and doctors over there, and to tell you the truth, I need more of a challenge than just to look after older people."

"If you're deciding that you're tired of what you're doing, then retire love, you don't need to work anymore, have more leisure time for yourself, there's no need to take up further challenges."

Amanda walked up to him and for a brief moment remembered that he did after all care about her. He was sitting on the bed putting his socks on and she stood above him looking down at his concerned, good looking features. For once she felt like the reasoner in the relationship. She took his face in her hands and looked into his eyes as she spoke to reassure him.

"Honey I know you may be worried, but I'll be fine. They've been doing this forever, taking groups of professionals over on a bus, everyone goes together, stay's together and comes back together. It's completely safe, I'm not going into a war zone, it's just Mexico."

She kissed him on the forehead. "Nina and I have been brushing up on our Spanish. Adios!", she said and walked out. "I'll see you at dinner."

"Who's NIna?"

"A new colleague at work. She's really nice and she's signed up too." She raised her voice as she skipped down the stairs.

Neil couldn't help but notice that she seemed excited by the new venture, and he knew she needed some form of stimulus in her life, so although he disliked the aspect of danger her volunteering held, he was proud of her and he would support her decision.

He shouted down the stairs to her, "I'm proud of you!"

But she heard him mutter under his breath, "Mexico *is* a war zone."

She smiled and slammed the front door.

Amanda had never been to Mexico, it was not a destination Neil would have considered an appropriate place to visit for his family, and Amanda was excited that she had found something positive that she could do on her own. Anyway she wasn't alone, a new nurse at work that Amanda had become friends with, had volunteered also, and so they agreed to go together and look after eachother.

Amanda and Nina waited at the bus stop for the volunteer bus to pick them up and they felt like schoolgirls going on a school camp. Nina hadn't been to Mexico either and so it was quite exciting for both of them. Once they were on the bus they looked around and calmed down as the other volunteers were composed.

"First time?" A large lady turned around from the seat in front of them.

"Yes, could you tell?"

"You can always tell the newbies. But believe me your excitement won't last. Not when you see what we're going into. But it will be worth it." She smiled knowingly and turned back around.

Amanda and NIna looked at each other dubiously.

She was not wrong.

Because Amanda and NIna only wanted to go on day trips to volunteer, they were assigned to a medical station in Tijuana, just across the border. The site in Colonia Obrera was a slum, thousands of shanty houses built on the side of a massive garbage dump. Here the families who lived in these tiny, dirty huts went to work in the garbage, looking for anything they could collect to earn a bit of money to buy a bit of food for the day. They would look for anything that could be recycled, cans, bottles, anything made of plastic, aluminium or metal. If they collected a huge bag full of recyclables they would earn ten dollars. Enough to buy some rice, beans or tortillas for the scant meal of the day.

Amanda and Nina were shocked at the conditions these

people lived in but they didn't have time to dwell on it as the people were waiting before they'd even arrived, and the endless line of women and children had already started to form outside the tent. Once inside each person recieved various medical tests such as blood pressure, diabetes screening, pregnancy tests, immunisations, baby health checks, etc. Food and clothing were also distributed at the same time, and the people were really very poor. It was an eye opener for Amanda and Nina and they returned home very tired, but very humbled and grateful for what they had at home.

The next time they alighted the bus to go to Colonia Obrera they were more pensive. They knew there was nothing intriguing about going there, it was just hard work and depressing scenes of people living on the edge.

They didn't talk anymore on the way but just looked out the window, comfortable in the thought that they had some kind of responsibility to help these people, that for some circumstances beyond their control, had to live in a makeshift tin shed above a massive garbage dump.

Amanda was lost in her own thoughts and she felt some inexplicable anger over the inequality in the world. People who lived just a few miles apart could have such a different standard of living and it just wasn't right. There was no point discussing it with anyone, everyone knew it wasn't right, but the argument would just become political and then no one got anywhere.

As soon as they arrived the families started lining up at the breakfast tent and then they would move on to the medical tent. It was a long day with only a lunch break and Amanda and NIna spent their break time just talking to the families that were there. By the afternoon they had only gotten through half the line and they felt the pressure to try and see everyone who needed attention.

A young medic volunteer brought in coffees and they sipped them greedily in between crying babies and the tired eyes of mothers who lived in constant stress. Suddenly they all heard the loud pop! pop! pop! of a gun going off and they rushed out of the tent to see where it came from. A middle aged man was lying bleeding on the yellow sand of the road. He'd been shot three times in the stomach. Two young men ran off up the hill and disappeared in between the tin houses. The medics wrapped the wound and then piled him into a car and a local doctor drove him to the nearest hospital. They were told later that he had survived the attack.

Everyone went back to work as if nothing had happened. It was the life in Mexico.

THE NEW PATIENT

"We have a new patient in your wing Amanda."
Barbara Fulton was the head nurse and she pulled no punches with the job. She was a tall woman with a bun wound tightly on the top of her head, making her seem even taller, and she would peer down her nose at you through her silver framed spectacles. She was intimidating to say the least, and would fire a nurse before they finished mouthing their excuses. Her facility had to be 'ship shape', as she called it, at all times, and it was a new and naïve person who would feel the brunt of her wrath if they should fail to keep to her exacting standards.

"This is her chart, read it thoroughly and then file it. Arriving 2.00pm." She held it out and was already walking quickly away, holding the chart backwards as if it was a baton in a relay race.

"Yes ma'am", Amanda had to run to catch up to her and receive the baton into her outstretched hand.

As Charge Nurse, Amanda made sure the room and bed were made up by the RN's and/or the LPN's, and ready for the new patients arrival, and was on hand at two o'clock to oversee that it all went smoothly. The avoidance of any interaction with the head nurse was always a good thing.

The new patient was an elderly Mexican woman by the name of Carmen Martinez. Her chart read that she was sixty four years old, but that she had been diagnosed with mild schizophrenia in her early thirties and had been in and out of psychiatric hospitals for a number of years. Now with only one remaining relative, her son, who was unable to care for her full time, she was being admitted as a permanent patient. Her medical conditions were being successfully managed with medication and her most recent admissions had been problem free.

"This should be a trouble free one," Amanda thought to herself. She liked it when the patients settled into their routine and became familiar with their carers. They then became more at home and began to accept their situation. Some settled down quicker than others, and then there were ones that never quite got used to being away from their family and the home that they'd lived in for up to fifty years in some cases. It was a huge wrench for them to suddenly be cast into an environment of strangers, medical staff and noise, constant noise, people coming and going; but those who accepted their situation fared the best.

Mrs. Martinez seemed quiet and compliant during her admission and she sat by the window quietly while Amanda checked that her belongings were filed and the bed was freshly made. Everything seemed in order and Amanda walked over to the window to welcome her newest arrival. She bent down slightly to look at Mrs. Martinez' face and get her attention.

"Hello Mrs. Martinez, I am Amanda, your head nurse, how are you?"

Mrs. Martinez looked up smiling. "This is nice", she said. Amanda assumed that she was referring to her room and she decided to go with that unless otherwise instructed.

"Yes it's a wonderful facility and we hope you will be happy here. Are you feeling up to a tour? I would like to show you the common room where you can make friends with the other residents and which also has a kitchen, dining and lounge area which backs onto the outdoor gardens. Do you feel up to that or would you prefer to wait until you've settled in a bit?"

Amanda knew that some patients responded well to the normality of making their own tea and coffee and spending time in the gardens, walking or sitting in the sunshine, while others were either too ill or not inclined to venture out of their rooms very often.

"No thank you dear, I'll just stay here for a little while." She remained smiling the whole time Amanda was speaking as if at some private joke, but Amanda was well accustomed to unusual behaviour. The small lady spoke with a heavy Mexican accent and Amanda knew from her records that she was from South America, not a native North American. The Mexican and Spanish illegal immigrants were a huge problem for the country but Amanda was never the type to discriminate. She treated all her patients fairly and equally, it wasn't her job to be political, and she actively distanced herself from political conversations, a favourite topic of her fathers. Her father had been an outspoken racist man and he and Neil had enjoyed many debates while he was still alive over the services accorded to illegal immigrants.

The thought of her father, of whom Amanda detested, unconsciously made Mrs. Martinez more endearing to her. She bent down again and patted Mrs. Martinez on the arm in a warm, familiar gesture. "That's fine Mrs. Martinez," she smiled warmly in return. "I'll come and look in on you again tomorrow. If you need anything just press the large red buzzer here and a nurse will be in here straight away. See you tomorrow, and again, welcome to your new home."

For some reason being nice to Mrs. Martinez made Amanda feel light headed. She smiled as broadly as the Mexican lady had as she walked out of the room.

Amanda had started her shift early, eager for the day to run smoothly, as she was expected promptly after work by her Muslim friends at the temple. She walked briskly through every room, greeting the patients while expertly surveying every detail, imagining she was looking through the Nurse Managers' eyes for any faults. Her small team followed behind her, rectifying any small anomaly she found. The morning past quickly and without incident, a rarity in a large facility of one hundred and thirty residents at any given time.

Amanda was about to go to lunch and she was starting to feel that this day was going to be one where everything ran smoothly, when she heard a loud raucous in the entrance way. She could hear a man's voice shouting loudly, and the quiet tone of the nurses trying to calm him.

She ran over to see what the problem was before the Head Nurse heard.

"What's going on here?" She asked one of the nurses trying to calm a large man, probably in his early fifties.

"He just came in and started yelling, and I can't get a word in!" The young nurse was flustered and Amanda patted her on the arm.

"I'll take over, don't worry." She turned to the robust man pacing before her.

"Can I help you Sir?"

There was something in Amanda's stature that made him take notice.

"I'm looking for my mother! I was told she was brought here but I can't find her!"

"Alright, we'll find her for you. I know every single mother that is brought in here so I'll be able to tell you exactly where she is." Amanda smiled a warm smile. "What is your mother's name?"

"Carmen, Carmen Martinez!" Frank bellowed as if he was shouting to someone across a huge room.

"Yes, your mother was just admitted yesterday, I'll take you straight to her." She kept smiling while taking his arm and steering him down the hall towards the wing where his mother's room was, talking all the while. If she kept chatting while they were moving it would calm him and dispel his anxiety.

"My name is Amanda, and I'm the charge nurse, and I looked in on your mother this morning, she's very comfortable, you

have no reason to worry about her at all. We will take the best
care of her, and you can visit her anytime you like. What is
your job, Mr. Martinez?"

"I work at the shipyard."

Frank was somehow soothed by Amanda's sweet voice and
he let her lead him down the hall.

"I make ship parts."

"That is so interesting, how long does it take to build a ship Mr.
Martinez?"

"Ah my name is Frank, just call me Frank."

"Alright Frank, I can see we're going to get along just fine."

Frank began to enjoy visiting his mother in the nursing home
because the nurses were all so nice to him. They looked
pleased to see him and always greeted him excitedly and he
didn't know anywhere else that did that. He thought maybe
they were just being polite but he didn't care, they always had
a kind word to say to him, and it made him feel good.

And Amanda, the charge nurse, she was the boss of the
place, she always had time to sit down and talk to him and his
mother.

On sunny days they would wheel her out into the pretty
garden with all the roses between the lawn and the road, and
they would sit chatting about anything and nothing, and it
would fill his day with hope.

He would work all week and visit his mum at ten o'clock on
the dot every Saturday and Amanda would sometimes be
waiting for him at the desk. They would walk towards his
mother's room and while Amanda spoke he would just listen,
and look at her, grunting now and then, and this became a
routine.

When Amanda spoke to Frank she found out what little he
told her about his life, and she realised he must be a very
lonely man. It was unlikely he would marry at his age and she

could see the lonely years that he must dread, stretching in front of him, and she felt sorry for him.

She spoke to the other nurses and asked them to always greet him when they saw him, and she made a point to spend time with him and his mother when she could.

It was a small thing she could do for a lonely pair and she saw it as part of her job.

There were so many sad people in the world. They were just two of them.

THE HOLIDAY

Neil decided the family needed a holiday. Actually he was worried about Amanda, she seemed distant and troubled, how long had she been like that? He hadn't noticed until recently and he realised that he hadn't paid much attention to her feelings for a long time. It was the great atrophy of being married for so long, you lose the ability to see and hear the other person. The truth was he had suddenly started listening to her and hearing that he was always the optimist, and she just didn't see life the same way. He was annoyed with himself for not seeing before what was so obvious to him now. He came to a realisation that this problem with Amanda may be serious and he did need to take notice finally.

He'd been listening to her now for quite a few weeks and he was suddenly alarmed at the way she was talking. The truth was she wasn't talking much at all and when she did she had nothing positive or contributory to say. She hardly interacted with them, just sort of acted like a sounding board for whatever anyone else was saying, but when he looked at her she really didn't seem to be listening to the person who was speaking. She would be looking out the window or busying herself at the sink or the dishwasher, not making eye contact either. He decided to look up the symptoms of clinical depression when he went to work that day. Could she be suffering from depression and he hadn't realised it? He had no idea how long it had been going on.

He tried talking to her but he found to his surprise that she wasn't open to talking to him. About anything. All of a sudden he realised there was a great big wall between them. And the wall was so high that he could not see a way over it. How had this happened? How long had there been this rift between them and why hadn't he realised this before?

Now for Neil this created a whole new set of problems. He was a perfectionist and took a great deal of pride in how his life and his family had turned out. He believed that he had created this perfect world that they all lived in, and of course everyone played their part in the formation and the continuation of their happy lifestyle but within himself he believed he was the creator and the sustainer of their world. So if Amanda was depressed where had he gone wrong? He wasn't too ignorant to realise that she had not had the greatest relationship with her parents or her sister but he'd always tried to make sure her life with him at home was a warm and loving one.

After reflecting on their life together with the two boys, and considering that the boys were happy and successful in what they were doing, he knew he had succeeded in that, so he decided the problem must be with Amanda's thinking. And being the man he was he decided that it was his responsibility to fix things. He may not have been listening in the past but he would definitely start listening to her now.

It had been a while since they had had a holiday together as a family and Neil thought a change of scenery with just the four of them would give them a chance to connect with each other again and give Amanda a chance to refocus on them as her supporters, or at least to remind her that they were always there for her. He thought that her family had always been her grounding and he hoped some time away with the three of them would help her to open up to him about how she was feeling. Perhaps then she might consider some professional help. After all if it really was depression she would need some outside counselling to get through it.

It never occurred to him that depression might be a life sentence for Amanda. He was the eternal optimist and saw every problem with a beginning, a fix-it, and an end. He saw Amanda's depression the same way. He thought they'd go on a holiday, she'd open up to him, they'd get some help for her, she'd recover and get back to her normal self, and then they'd continue on in their happy future. It was impossible for him to see it any other way. Not only did he have no clinical knowledge of depression but it would destroy his whole perception of their lives together, their past, their present, and their future. In short he would be a destroyed man. So he decided to take control of the situation and a holiday was his answer.

At first Amanda and the boys were resistant but he wouldn't give in and his persistence in persuading them to go paid off. It had been a long time since they had gone on a real holiday and this time they would go to Hawaii. They'd never been there, although they'd talked about it a few times, and it wasn't so far that they'd have to take extra time off work. They'd get there in a couple of hours and be able to enjoy the holiday for the maximum amount of time; a whole week to connect as a family again. Neil took on the job of arranging the holiday as his project, a gift to the family that he had perhaps taken for granted for a while, and he became excited by the idea. It was still two months away before all of them could get time off together but he made all the bookings and couldn't stop talking about it.

The others didn't share his enthusiasm.

Aaron and Luke were not overly thrilled with the idea of a holiday. Aaron did not want to take time away from his studies even if he was on mid year break, and he didn't have enough time with his girlfriend Veronica as it was. Just thinking about her stirred up feelings he could hardly keep under control. He wanted to touch her all the time and when they kissed he felt a warm happy feeling. But she was a good girl, and they had never gone past kissng. Once he attempted to touch her soft breast with his hand but she pulled away indignantly and refused to see him for a week. He promised not to do it again and they went back to being constant companions, before school, in class, and after school. Which was why it was such a shame that his Mum did not approve of Veronica. She thought they spent way too much time together, and though it was true, he wished Mum would ease up on it. She nagged him repeatedly not to bring her over all the time but she had an alcoholic father so she preferred not to go home till late if she could help it. After Veronica left, the constant arguing would start. "Doesn't she have a home to go to? Why is she always here? Can't you have break from her for a little while?" Aaron knew it was no use arguing; when it came to Veronica, his Mum only saw black and white, no colours. He would just say "Leave me alone Mum!", and slam the door behind him as he went to his room.

He hated upsetting his mum, they were very close, but lately they just couldn't see eye to eye about anything. They hardly ever argued but Mum would give him the silent treatment just like she did to Dad if she wasn't happy with him. It was not a good idea to let that go on for too long, otherwise Dad would get involved and the whole family would have to sit down for a "talk". Aaron and Luke avoided the talk like the plague, it was like going back to primary school, and Mum and Dad had a way of making them divulge much more than they had originally intended, which would then result in super consequences. So the boys usually found a way to compromise with their Mum, who after a few days could be more easily manipulated into decreasing the particular subjects importance.

But with Veronica it was different. Aaron was surprised and disappointed by the way his Mum regarded her. He'd always had the loving support of both his parents in everything he put his mind to and she'd never acted this way before with any of his friends, male or female. But when he'd started bringing Veronica home alone, his Mum actively avoided her and therefore made everyone feel uncomfortable. Suddenly there were strict rules in the house, no one here at dinner, no one who wasn't family allowed in the house after dinner and taking Veronica anywhere upstairs was strictly forbidden. Veronica was cool about it and she did nothing to inflame the situation but for the first time that he could remember, Aaron was in constant conflict with his Mum. And for the first time he could remember there was a constant source of contention in his home.

Sometimes after dinner he would hear Mum and Dad arguing about him and Veronica in the kitchen or the study, sometimes even in their room at night. He was upset that he was the source of the discord in the house but he didn't know what to do about it. He certainly wasn't going to break up with Veronica just to please his Mum when she was being unreasonable. After all they never did anything wrong, they really just hung out together.

He made sure that the relationship didn't affect his school work so that Mum had no fuel to get her way, but deep down it upset him. He was torn between wanting to spend as much time as possible with Veronica and not doing anything that would cause a rift to form between himself and his Mum.

When Dad suggested the holiday he was at first horrified. He'd formed some loose plans for himself, Veronica and his friends for the holidays and didn't want to cancel them to spend more time with his family.

One morning he was voicing his objections quite emphatically when his father took him by the arm and quietly pulled him into the adjoining room.

"Look Aaron, I know this may be not the most convenient time for us to get away together but I know that your Mum needs this. I think we need this as a family. Take my word for it your Mum is feeling like we're not much of a family anymore, do you understand? This would be the best thing for her right now."

"Is this one of Mum's ideas to get me away from Veronica again?"

"No I promise this was my idea, she had nothing to do with it. Promise me you"ll give me your full support with this, I really need this from you right now, Aaron."

Aaron could tell by the serious tone in his Dad's voice that he was not going to sway from this course.
"Ok Dad, I'll do it, but you're right, it's not a great time for me."

Neil made sure they made the plane on time, and as he sat holding his wife's hand in the comfortable seat of business class he looked out of the window without seeing. He knew that this trip was the best thing he'd done for his family for a long time and it would restore the close bond they'd always had. It was perhaps the last holiday they would have together as just the four of them, with the boys growing up so quickly, and so he wanted it to be memorable.

He'd decided to spend more than he originally intended to make sure that Amanda really got the rest that she needed. It would be luxury from the word go, with the hotel in Kauai offering the best in relaxation and a lavish spa for Amanda to relish in. As for the kids they were old enough to find activities for themselves, and with snorkelling, bike riding, zip lining, buggies, surfing, kayaking and of course swimming, and lots of others on offer, they could find their own ways to have fun. He would spend his time making sure that Amanda was pampered and relaxed and then maybe she would open up to him about how she's been feeling.

Neil was a self assured man. His childhood was idyllic with just himself and his younger brother growing up with professional parents who were kind and supportive. His parents encouraged good study practices and independence and in reward the children received gifts and holidays around the world.

His brother Matthew went into Business and Marketing and travelled around the world as a CEO for different companies, but Neil was happy to stay in the domestic market. He had no global ambitions like his brother, and he was awarded Professor of Social Sciences at The University of California after fifteen years of research, study and lecturing at various institutions around the country. He had a quiet, studious and kind personality compared to his brother and other men his age and it bode him well in his career, but the same could not be said with the subject of women. Being a studious man, he had his head in his books for a long time and therefore it was difficult for him to begin relationships with women and start dating, and he was well into his thirties before he met Amanda.

He had dated a few women close to his own age and was seeing one in particular regularly when he first met her. Like many of the female students on the campus he knew she was attracted to him, it was a common thing for them to be attracted to Professors, a status thing, and he was always flattered but circumspect; not only were women of her age young and impressionable, he didn't want to ruin his reputation as a responsible figure at the University. His immediate peers would not look favorably on that.

So initially he made sure that any interpretation of his interest in her was false. After lectures she would make it a point of asking him questions, as would other students, but he found she had a real capacity for understanding, and he was drawn to her caring nature. He therefore spent a lot of time discussing and debating with her, and they started to form a precarious bond.

Neil was a caring and generous person and therefore had a loving and successful relationship with his girlfriend and they spent a lot of time travelling and enjoying each other's company. But he couldn't help feeling that there wasn't really a spark between them and he could see them growing old and boring too quickly.

As it came closer to the time that Amanda would inevitably be leaving her studies and starting her career, he decided to ask her out. He had been single for a few months after ending his relationship and found himself becoming stressed about no longer having Amanda in his life. He'd come to the realisation that despite her being over a decade younger than himself, she was very mature, and he could see her fitting into his life. She wasn't overly ambitious, like himself, and he was impressed with her caring nature. She reminded him of his mother. He never told her that, but he thought it was a good trait.

They began regularly having coffee together and it then progressed to dinner and they easily became a couple. She didn't seem to mind spending time with his older friends and she was the perfect host to his business associates and aquantances.

Their families got on well together on the rare occasions that they met, and after their small but opulent wedding, he could not have asked for a more perfect wife.

After the boy's were older she continued her career in nursing and he thought they had the perfect life, and he wasn't far wrong. Until recently there had not been any significant hurdles in their life, and other than Amanda's parents both passing away within the space of a few years, they had lived life pretty unscathed by the standards of the world.

He did not discount that the passing of her parents must have had some affect on her, but because she wasn't really close to anyone in her family, he thought she had handled it well, and could not see any lasting implications of the events. Perhaps it had affected her more than he thought, and he really wanted to communicate with her better during this holiday than he had been doing in recent times.

Amanda seemed to respond well to the holiday. She finally seemed a bit relaxed and would even laugh and joke with the boys at dinner time. She was not adverse to any of the treatments he had booked for her, like massage and spa treatments, and when she returned from these services she glowed. They were warm and loving to each other and their relationship seemed to be back on track.

On the third morning she returned to him into their private cabin after one of her treatments and she lay next to him on the bed where he was reading.
"You know darling, I was really against this when you first came up with the idea, but I can honestly say it's the best idea you've had for a long time." She smiled disarmingly, and he saw again the girl he'd first noticed in school twenty years ago.
She reached over and kissed him lovingly and longingly on the lips, "Thank you, you've always been my hero."

He took her in his arms and slowly and lovingly disrobed her. They hadn't felt like this for a long time and he couldn't have been a happier man.

Amanda felt like a changed woman. At first she had vocally protested about accepting Neils idea of the family going on a holiday together, but she couldn't have been more wrong about it. It had done them all a world of good, and had recemented them as a family.
She was always impressed with what Neil could do to solve all the families problems, and again he had not failed them this time.
They had spent every evening together with the boys, after

Aaron and Luke had an active time together doing whatever teenage boys do on a holiday. The boys' seemed to get on well for a change and seemed happy. The four of them laughed and talked at the dinner table, and afterwards sat at the pool in the waning heat of the day. They bonded again like they hadn't for years and the feeling of a strong family unit was again shared by them all.

Amanda decided to apologise to Aaron about Veronica. They walked arm in arm along the beach in the twilight and she brought up the subject.

"I'm really sorry about the way I've acted over you and Veronica."

"Thanks, Mum." Aaron was genuinely touched, and hugged his mum.

"Wait, I'm not finished." She smiled at her oldest son, he was such a good boy. He had never been rebellious at all, Luke was different, but Aaron was so steadfast, so trustworthy, just like his Dad.

"I want you to know that I've always trusted you, and believed whatever you've said. You're a good boy, you've respected our rules and respected Veronica, it's just the way you are." She tousled his hair and he ran off for a bit.

"Come here!" She pulled him back.

"I promise I'll be much nicer to her when we get back, she must be a lovely girl if she's interested in you."

"Thanks Mum, you're going to really like her, just wait and see."

They'd caught up to Neil and Luke who were walking in front.

"I'm proud of you." Neil gave Amanda a kiss on the lips.

"Honey, I'm sure you've noticed but I may be struggling with a bit of depression. I just want you to know that I'm going to get some help when we return. It's nothing to worry about, and you were right, this holiday was the best thing for me right now. Thank you so much, it's been wonderful."

"I'm so glad to hear that, I've been worried about you." Neil hugged his wife close as they dug their toes into the soft sand.

"Well don't, I'll get it sorted."
The soft golden glow of the disappearing sun hovered gently
on the horizon, and then the dark sky and first twinkling of
stars heralded the final night of their holiday.
 They turned and slowly walked back towards the hotel.

FRANK'S MELTDOWN

Frank didn't usually read the local paper. He usually just threw it straight into the bin. He knew that paper's were just about politics, that's what his Dad always said anyway. He would sit at the small metal and laminate kitchen table and bang his fist on the table while he was eating, saying "Damn politics!", and pieces of food would spray all over the paper. Frank was never good at reading anyway and although over the years he learnt to read a lot of sentences, he could never read a long paragraph or story.

But today there was something on the front page that caught his eye. He saw it just as he was about to push it into the bin under the sink in the old kitchen of his mother's house. He had lived in this house on and off for fifty years and he was as much a part of it as that old metal table.

It was a house that was owned by the city and like all the public housing in the area it was run down. The city left the upkeep to the current tenants and because his mother had been in and out of the house centred around her hospital admissions, and then he took over the tenancy when she died, nothing had been updated in all of that time. Frank didn't know how to do any repairs, and he really didn't care what the house looked like anyway; it was a roof over his head and that was it.

There was a lot of history of Frank's family in that house. He'd lived there since he could remember, and his mother and father had lived and died while staying there. These days the house was always empty but there had been some tumultous times here in the past. When all the uncles and cousins and friends were in the house when he was young it was an exciting place, full of exotic smells and loud noise.

Today it was a lonely dilapidated house and all Frank had was
the memories. He ate and slept there, and that was the extent
of his connection with it.

In the morning he would stand under the old rusty shower
head for five minutes and then move to the kitchen, where he
would stir some leftover beans on the electric stove, plop them
onto a grilled tortilla and that was breakfast. On Sunday he
might fry a couple of eggs and throw them on top with tomato
sauce. In the evening he'd have some hot bean mix with
mince and chillies or a hot spicy pasta or rice soup with
breadrolls or tortillas. It didn't vary much as Frank was not
much of a cook.

Frank lived a lonely life these days and it didn't look like
changing. He was an old man at fifty, set in his ways, the old
ways of long past, and the world outside had overtaken him
and left him behind. There was nothing and no one to pull him
into the present, and he went about his business invisiby to
the world around him, and he liked it that way. He was stuck in
the past and could not have changed his behaviours if he
wanted to.

At night before he went to bed he would watch a little bit of tv
on the old set that his mother bought in one of her lucid
periods, which could last anywhere from days to a couple of
months. She would take him shopping and buy him a treat
without telling his father who did not believe in wasting money,
and who certainly did not believe that Frank should be the
recipient of anything bought with that money. But his mother
loved him in those times and she would buy him a treat like a
sweet or his favorite, a chocolate churro. He would replay
those shopping trips over and over in his mind. They were the
only happy memories he could recall, other than with Rosie
but he'd long ago blocked them out of his mind. He could not
deal with remembering anything whatsoever about her.

When he'd seen the news and the replays of the twin tower
destruction on his little television set, he would walk around
the house in a rage, banging his hand into the thin asbestos

walls, adding holes to the many that had appeared over the years. He hated the Muslims more than any other race, and he wished he could kill them all.

Today he was about to screw up the paper and throw it in the bin as he did every Friday after breakfast, but he saw something out of the corner of his eye and he carefully unfolded it again with his big clumsy fingers. Spread out on the front page was a picture of the new Muslim families that had moved into the neighborhood recently and he banged his fist so hard on the paper that he put a crack in the old, wasted laminate of the table. He then tore the paper into a million pieces and burned it in the bin, filling the room with smoke and acrid smells. He wished he could burn the Muslims. If he was still with the gang they would never let Mozzies move into this neighborhood, but the days were gone when the gang controlled who moved in and who didn't. There was no control anymore and he could do nothing about it.

He went to work in a foul mood and drank extra hard that night at the Star Hotel, where he'd been drinking for thirty years.

When Frank checked the mail at the old rusty letter box attached to the broken and cracked concrete fence at the front of his house, he would throw away anything that he didn't recognize as a bill. He did not like reading and he did not like letters, and he hated opening a letter just to find out that it was an advertisement for someone selling something, or some information not relevant to him at all, and so he got into the habit of throwing everything away that he did not assign into the bill pile. He hated owing money and he would not be late with paying a bill and so as soon as he got one in the mail, he would walk to the post office and pay it on the spot. That way he avoided strange people contacting him and harrassing him and enabled his life to run relatively inconspicously and insignificantly for the most part.

But at times his habit of throwing away letters got him into trouble as he would miss some important information that might affect him.

This was one such time. Although the city had been sending him consecutive letters warning him that new areas of public housing were being built and old areas were being put up for demolition and private sale, he did not read these letters. He did not read the letter that explained to him that his house was one that was affected by the decision, and that he had been invited to apply for new housing in a nearby neighborhood. So he did not have any warning that his house was being demolished and that he would have to move.

One day there was a loud knocking on his door. It was Saturday evening and he had just returned from his usual Saturday routine of the nursing home and then the pub. He'd been watching tv, flicking stations and he always had a Bud before going to bed; he sat slumped on the old dirty couch with a beer in his hand.

At first he ignored the knocking, but after a while it turned into more of a pounding and he heard the voice of the local lieutenant.

"Open up Frank!"

The coppers were now shining lights in the windows through the gaps in the curtains so he had to get up and answer the door.

"Ok, I'm coming!" he bellowed, as he stiffly got up from the sofa. The tv was loud, and he went and turned the sound dial to off.

He opened the squeaky door and there stood the lieutenant and another officer he hadn't seen before.

"What the fuck do you want?" Frank was never happy to see the police.

"We've been coming around for a couple of weeks Frank, haven't caught you before." The lieutenant could smell the stench of alcohol on Frank's breath, and was not looking forward to this confrontation.

The local police knew Frank well. Most of their members had had some form of interaction with him at some point over the years, and while he'd been in serious trouble in his younger years, he'd narrowly avoided serious jail time and had since become merely another local drunk. They knew he was occasionally involved in fights at the local pub, but other than that he kept to himself.

"Frank, I'm sorry to give you this but we have an eviction notice to serve on you." He thought he'd start off with a polite tactic.

"What, what is it?" Frank had drank a lot of hard stuff that night and had barely made it home, stumbling and tripping all the way. He had sobered a bit since half watching tv and half passing out on the couch, but he still wasn't coherent or understanding.

"It's an eviction notice Frank. The house is being demolished and you have to move. Did you get the letters?"

"What letters?"

"The letters telling you that you have to move out Frank. The house is being demolished. You have to find somewhere else to live. Sorry Frank, you've only got two weeks left here."

"Two weeks?" Frank still wasn't comprehending what the lieutenant was saying.

"Yes Frank, listen. You have two weeks then you've gotta be out. Here's the notice, read it, if you have any problems, call the city. See ya Frank. I'll come back next week, make sure you're out ok. Seeya." He handed Frank the notice and with that the two policemen turned and walked off.

The next morning Frank was in a temper. He'd gone to bed after the policemen left and slept deeply through the night but in the morning he remembered them coming and what they'd said.

He had no idea what to do and where he would go and he just lumbered around the house banging his fist into the walls.

The next week was a nightmare for Frank. He went to work

in a daze, and though he followed the same routines as he usually did, they were mixed with a feeling of panic and uncertainty and he had no way of coping.

His sleep patterns became so erratic that he would wake up repeatedly during the nights and he became constantly irritable, more than normal.

Frank could not accept that he had to leave his home, the home he had lived in since he was born except for a few years at his cousins', and so instead of organising himself to leave he did nothing. He would go to work and to the pub in a state of unconscious panic and the few who spoke to him, found him to be nonsensical. He would blabber out words quickly if he had to and then move off.

The Saturday when he went to see his mother Amanda was not standing at the desk to meet him. He asked the receptionist where she was and she told him she'd gone on holiday for a week. She'd be back next week, he could talk to her then.

He wheeled his mother out into the sun but today was a day that she didn't recognise him.

"Who are you? Who are you?" She kept saying.

It had been a long time since Frank had cried but that day he wheeled her behind a tree where no one could see and he cried in her lap, huge throbbing sobs that came from somewhere deep inside him.

On Monday morning Frank stepped out of his front door to go to work and there was a Muslim family standing outside his house. He could tell they were Muslims because they spoke in a strange arabic language and the woman and her daughter had scarves on their heads.

"What the hell do you want?!" He bellowed at them.

"Ah sorry, we are just looking at the neighborhood, we are

looking to buy some land here, sorry." And they started to move off.

"No fuckin mozzies are buying this house!" Frank stood on the pavement glaring at them until they hurried around the corner out of sight.

The idea of the one race that he hated the most living anywhere near the house that he treasured was more than Frank could bear and that night Frank devised a plan. He would punish all the Mozzies who thought they could come in and take over his neighborhood, he would give retribution for 9/11, and he would be the vindicator who defended the pride of the Americans.

He needed to do something to show the intruders that they were not welcome around here and they better get lost, and he remembered exactly how to do it. He knew exactly what he had to do, he'd done it many times before.

He slept better that night and woke up in the morning with a new purpose. He rummaged to the back of wardrobe and found his old black hoodie that he used to wear when he was young. He pulled it over his head and instantly felt like he was back there. He reached back behind a broken panel and pulled out some items he hadn't seen in years. He stroked them lovingly and found an old rag to clean them up. Then he made his usual breakfast and walked out the door.

<u>NINA</u>

Tomorrow Amanda was meeting a friend. Her name was Nina and she was a new nurse that Amanda had quickly hit it off with, and they had become firm friends ever since. A lot of the other nurses Amanda worked with, were either older or younger than herself, or their personalities or life circumstance were just too different than her own, and so she never had become good friends with any of them. But with Nina it was different. Straight away Amanda had recognised that Nina held the same values sacred as she did, such as family values, honesty, an openness that did not lend itself to false deceit or false showing off. And although Nina was much younger than herself, they built a rapport that quickly developed. She had a warmth that Amanda was attracted to, that was lacking in her own family and friends, and when Nina spoke of her family, and the care and closeness they had for each other, she felt an admiration and envy that she could not dispel. Amanda wished that she could be part of that wonderful large family, made up of Nina's brother, her sister, her mother and father who were wealthy and happy, and guided their children to be successful in their lives, with love support along the way. Nina explained that her family had told her that she would always be supported financially if she needed it, and to prosper in her future. Amanda was so envious when she heard this, she couldn't imagine parents helping their children financially, her own parents had never offered, and she felt awe at the closeness that Nina obviously had with her family. Amanda encouraged Nina to talk about her family and Nina happily obliged, sharing with Amanda for hours all the intimate details of her family life. She also spoke of her boyfriend of two and a half years, and how her parents expected her to marry early. Nina had a maturity and understanding way beyond her years and Amanda felt a trust and security in her that she had not experienced before.

So tomorrow Amanda was on a mission. She had been feeling lately that she was such a failure in life, that her depression was getting the better of her and that she needed to get help before it became worse. She had determined to tell Nina, the only person she trusted, other than Neil, about how she'd been feeling. There were times like this when she sort of looked at herself from the outside, as if she was diagnosing someone else, and she knew that her isolation and depression were not good. She knew from being a nurse, that the first step in treatment was talking to someone, anyone you trusted, and they would usually give some clarity to the situation, then you could take the next step.

It had been a long time since Amanda trusted anyone and just the thought of now having someone that she could share her private feelings with gave her a touch of joy. She felt her spirit lifting already, realising that with making the decision to tell Nina how she'd been suffering from serious depression issues, that the hope of recovery was suddenly a possibility.

She knew it would not be easy. She would have to sit down with a counsellor or psychologist and wade through the circumstances of people, events, years of her life, that may have contributed to her troubled state of mind. She would then have to work on exercises designed to negate her negative self talk and develop again a peaceful and happy mindset. She knew all this from patients being treated over the years at the hospital, and she knew it was hard work and didn't always succeed. But she was feeling good about taking the first step.

It would probably take years. But she had made up her mind.

Amanda felt a bit of a spring in her step as she alighted off the train on her way to her Muslim friends and the synagogue.

Lately she had lost interest in the teachings, it never really gelled with her, she hung on to her belief in Christianity and she was getting tired of learning about the Qur'an when she believed the teachings of the Bible, but she cherished the friendships she had developed with Fatima and the other women. She was so grateful that they had been there in a very confusing time for her and their warm generosity and openness to a stranger humbled her. She would always have a place for them in her life.

These days she did not immaturely pretend to be a Muslim but she always wore a head scarf on her way to meet them and she was honored to do so. She may have not agreed with some of the things in their way of life, but then they felt the same way about hers, and they kept a mutual respect about them. At times they had heated discussions about some topics that were so different to each other but they always ended up hugging and respecting each other in the end.

Today she felt she had a clear mind and she resolved to tell Neil about her friends at the synagogue and the details about what she'd been doing there so often. Maybe he could even come along for some prayer; she'd always loved that about him, his open mind, and it had bode well for the children. He would be surprised at first but she hoped he would then take an interest in what had preoccupied a lot of her time over the last couple of years, when he knew she'd been distant and unhappy.

She was nearing the temple and instantly recognised her group of friends standing outside the front entrance. There were the older two women, Mahdiya and Ibtihaj, with their sharp click clicking tongue and authoritative way of speaking; there was shy thirtiesh Raytah, so timid for her age, only just learning that she could have a voice in discussions; Nerida, with the moody eyes and the clique culture, but with the warmest heart when she finally accepted you; Yaheenda, the sweetest young newlywed, only seventeen, (not for Amanda to judge), and of course Fatimah, Amanda's best friend, confidante, acting counsellor and guide in all things Muslim.

Looking at them she wondered why they had opened their hearts and their lives to her when she really had nothing to offer them except a morbid curiosity and immature loneliness, but they had sensed a need in her that they knew they could fulfil and without prejudice invited her into their world. She would be eternally grateful for their generosity of spirit, and she knew that somehow these strangers had helped her through a dark place.

She was nearly upon them and they turned toward her in greeting, and she was about to exclaim a warm hello, when she saw first Mahdiya and Raytah contort their bodies in a strange way and then fall to the ground, and straight after Yaheenda do the same. There were two young men standing near a car and Amanda saw them fall to the ground as well. She heard some loud cracks, like firecrackers going offf, and then she saw a man shouting from a car driving past them. She then felt a force push into her middle, and her legs buckled underneath her. She suddenly found it hard to breathe and realised she was laying on the hard concrete footpath unable to move. She felt something warm start to spread across her stomach and chest, it felt like warm water but she couldn't think where it may have come from.

She heard her voice being called from far away, then she thought she heard screaming, and Fatimah's face then came close to her own.

"Amanda!" "Amanda!" "Are you hurt?!" Her voice sounded stricken and Amanda wondered why. She tried to get up but nothing in her body would work.

Fatimah saw the immense amount of blood start to pool around Amanda's body and her words became softer.

"Amanda, hang on help is coming, I can hear the sirens". She smiled a beautiful warm smile and rubbed Amanda's hand incessantly. She wondered why she couldn't feel it but felt confused. Why did she have to hold on?

Her body then convulsed and she suddenly realised she'd

been shot, like Mahdiya and Nashida and Yaheenda had been.

"The others", she tried to nod to where the other women had been standing but couldn't lift her head. "Are they alright?" Fatimah shook her head, tears silently streaming down her brown cheeks; she did not want to look to where the others had been standing, "I don't know." She closed her eyes shaking her head for a long time.

"Amanda, we love you, you know", she said it in such a sombre way that Amanda became alarmed.

"I know, and I love you all, I am so grateful to you all, but there'll be time for that later." She smiled and then sharp pain gripped her body and made tears sting her eyes; she gasped for air but couldn't get any, and then Amanda Hendley was gone.

Fatimah felt Amanda's hand go limp in her grasp and she cried a loud wail into the chaotic, noisy air.

Frank Martinez was feeling elated as he poured the bullets all over the area in front of the Muslim temple. He finally felt vindicated for all the awful things the Muslims had done to him and to all Americans, and he felt that he would be the one who stood up and exclaimed loudly the injustices done to them. The bullets sprayed into people and he remembered the feelings he had of companionship and acceptance that he received every time he murdered or maimed someone as a member of the Logan Heights gang. It brought back good memories for him of family and friends, his mother and of Rosie. If only he could go back to that time, he would save her and their life together would have been good forever.

But he could not go back and all the frustration of the past twenty years of loneliness and bitterness and sorrow he poured out with the bullets that flailed out in front of him. He heard the crack, crack as they hit brick and concrete, and the

whak, whak when they hit their mark, a human body.
It was over quickly and he hastily pulled the rifle back into the
car and sped off down the road. But just before he did he
caught a glimpse of the eyes of his last victim, a woman with a
pale head scarf, walking alone towards the temple, waving to
the people standing outside. He felt suddenly confused and
her eyes seemed vaguely familiar. But he didn't have time to
think about it for long as he heard sirens coming closer and
then the police cars were upon him. They blocked him in front
and in the rear, and he gave up easily. He held his hands in
the air with a scowl on his face and then he was roughly pulled
out of the car and thrown to the ground. He heard the familiar
sound of steel and felt the cold pain as the cuffs were put on
his wrists behind his back. He was yanked up and thrown into
the police van.

But he was feeling ecstatic. He'd done what he came to do.
He'd found his purpose in life and he'd carried it out. His whole
life had been moving towards this pivotal point, he saw it all
so clearly now. He knew this time there was no getting out of
it. He'd go to jail a hero to all Americans. He couldn't wipe the
smile off his face.

Frank's elation at what he felt he'd achieved did not abate for
many days. He saw himself as a hero, and he was sure all
Americans would feel the same way about him. He felt he was
the sole defender of the people, delivering the vindication of all
Americans against the Muslims invading the country and
taking what did not belong to them. Those first few weeks in
jail were like a dream and he went through the motions in a
daze, and because he was in solitary confinement he did not

gain any insight from the other prisoners of what they thought of his assault.

Then one day after he'd been sentenced and was out of solitary, he was watching the small TV in the common room of the prison. There was a report about him and his attack on the Temple and they were showing the faces of the victims. He stood outwardly proud and smirking until he saw a face that he remembered. A hint of recognition flashed in his mind and he remembered the eyes of his last victim.

He saw a familiar face shown on the screen with her name. The name was Amanda Hendley. And then the full horror of what he'd done hit him with as much force as a bullet would have. He realised he'd killed the only person who'd ever been genuinely kind to him and his dear mother - his mother's nurse Amanda.

THE END.